KENTUCKY TIME

JAMES PLAYSTED WOOD

KENTUCKY TIME

JAMES PLAYSTED WOOD

Addison-Wesley

LIBRARY OF CONGRESS CATALOGING IN PUBLICATION DATA

Wood, James Playsted, 1905-
   Kentucky time.
   SUMMARY: Despite his parents' inattention, a young
boy enjoys growing up in Kentucky, mainly because of a
devoted and sensitive uncle.
   [1. Kentucky — Fiction. 2. Family life — Fiction.
3. Fathers and sons — Fiction] I. Title.
PZ7.W8496Ke   [Fic]   77-4383
ISBN 0-201-09344-8

Addison-Wesley Publishing Company, Inc.
Reading, Massachusetts 01867
Printed in the United States of America
ABCDEFGHIJK-WZ-7987

Jacket illustration and book design by
Charles Mikolaycak

for David C. Hardman and Donald Gordon Smith

KENTUCKY

Every year its springtime,
Leaves down in the fall,
Thoroughbreds in bluegrass.
Goldenrod. That's all.

Vergil Trewbridge

1

I KNEW WHAT MARGARET HOBART WAS GOING TO say as soon as I saw her on the old gray stone steps that go up between two of the big white pillars of our house.

Her face was red, and her eyes were blazing. She jumped up and down shaking her fists in the air and said, "I'm so mad I'm mad at everybody there is, and I wish there were more people in the world so I could be mad at them too!"

I've had whooping cough and the measles and the mumps, and all of them were bad, but cousins are worse, and Margaret Hobart is the worst of them all.

"Are you mad at me too?" I said.

"Of course not," said Margaret Hobart. "I only get mad at people, and you're just a little boy and don't count for anything."

I've heard her say that before too. I've known Margaret Hobart for ten years going on eleven because that's how old I am. She's twelve, but she's only known me for ten years so I don't think she's so much even if she is that much older than I am. I wouldn't want to spend two years being Margaret Hobart anyway.

"What are you mad about now?" I asked her.

Margaret Hobart dropped her fists and let her face turn back to its usual color. She brushed back her long hair, which is more brown than it is blonde, and looked at me as if she didn't like what she saw. She almost always looks at me that way.

"Oh, nothing today — yet. I'm just practicing."

"You don't need to," I said.

"You don't know anything about it. You don't know anything at all. You never did, and you never will. I'm so mad . . ."

I let her go on and just looked at her and didn't listen. Usually that's the best way with Margaret Hobart. She lives with her mother a piece down the road. Their house is pretty good, but it's brick, and it's smaller than ours, and it doesn't have any pillars. When I was little I used to think that Margaret Hobart was her full name, that Margaret was her first name and Hobart was her hind name and wondered why her mother called her Margaret Hobart. Then I found out that she has a different last name and Margaret Hobart is her first name. Probably it takes two names to handle her. Her father is usually in Atlanta or Nashville or Knoxville or some place, and I don't blame him.

"You say one more word to me, Verge Trewbridge, and I'll kill you!" said Margaret Hobart.

"I didn't say anything yet."

"You'd better not. I just dare you to! What do you want anyway?"

"I want to go into my own house, and I can't because you're in the way."

"If that isn't a nice way to address a southern lady," said Margaret Hobart in her sweetest voice. She slid her eyes — they're gray — around at me and shut them and opened them a couple of times very fast. Then she pulled her lips together and sniffed. Suddenly she gathered her skirts around her, which was pretty hard because she was wearing blue jeans, and started across the big lawn toward the road and her house.

I didn't go in right away even after she was gone because we live in Kentucky, and it's always good to look at so I looked at it again.

I don't ever tell all I know, and I'm not going to now, so I won't tell you just where we live in Kentucky. It would be a long walk — probably take you three days if you walked fast and didn't stop anywhere — to Cave Hill in Louisville where my grandfather is buried because he was an important man in Kentucky and used to play poker at the Seelbach with Marse Henry Watterson himself. We're just as far from the Big Sandy. Our town isn't as large as Lexington, but it's bigger than Danville or Frankfort, even if Frankfort is the capital. It's almost as old as Harrodsburg, and my family has always been in it. It's the prettiest part of Kentucky, and there were Trewbridges here even before Daniel Boone came in through the Cumberland Gap and down the Wilderness Road.

We don't live right in town but a piece out because that's where we've always lived. Our house goes away back. It was here long before the War Between the States, and it's in the guide books, and people come and look at it from the outside as if it were My Old Kentucky Home in Bardstown. I've seen that house, and I don't think too much of it even if our roof does leak in a couple of places when the rain slants from the north, and the lawns aren't close-clipped, and the redbuds need trimming and little things like that. We have bigger pillars on our house and rolling fields behind it and then our woods down by the river. Except my uncle's farm, it's the best there is.

The big hall was dark and cool when I went inside. The ceilings are very high, and the oak floor is almost black. I like it that way. That's why I usually come in the front door though I never tell anybody.

"Come in the front like company again. Can't use the back like family," said Miz Liz when I got to the kitchen.

"School bus doesn't come by the back," I said.

"Too lazy to walk a few steps," said Miz Liz.

"Saving my strength for when I get old," I said.

Miz Liz in ninety-one. She had some husbands, but they were mostly no-count, she says, and she's not going to get another unless she finds one that just suits.

I hope she never does because, if it were not for Miz Liz, I probably would never get anything to eat and have to go to school naked. She knows where my clothes are and keeps them clean but not so clean I'm uncomfortable. She has some children and grandchildren places like New Orleans and Charleston and Paducah. They send her things and cards at Christmas but not all of them because some of them are dead. The others are mostly no-count too, she says.

My Uncle Henry says he doesn't believe Miz Liz is ninety-one. He thinks she is a hundred and ninety-one because as far as he knows she has always lived in our family. He is forty-five, but he says he can remember back at least a hundred years because people were always telling him things about the past of Kentucky and our family, and he can't remember when Miz Liz wasn't around and looking just as tall and thin and stooped and sharp-eyed as she is now.

"There," said Miz Liz. She put down a plate with a big fried chicken leg and some pickles and a glass of milk and two brown sugar cookies. "Eat it up and don't make yourself sick."

"I don't want to be sick," I said.

"Boys are s'posed to eat till they get sick," said Miz Liz. "That's what makes them boys. Helps take the taste of school out of your mouth too. Want more you know where it is. I got better things to do than wait on boys track mud in the front door."

"There isn't any mud," I said.

"Was last winter," said Miz Liz, "and you did the same thing then."

You can't win arguments with women so I took a big bite out of the chicken leg, and it was tender and sweet, and then I took a long drink of milk, and it was cool and rich, good Jersey milk, high butter fat. I know because I know where we get it, and my Uncle Henry tells me these things.

"There's no one to home at our house, and I'm hungry," said Margaret Hobart. "Where's another chicken leg?" She'd come in the back door.

"This chicken only had two," I said, "and I ate the other one last night."

"Didn't your folks ever teach you not to be greedy? I'll have a cookie then." She took both of mine before I could stop her.

Miz Liz came back. She looked at Margaret Hobart. "There's homemade bread in the bread box and some good sumach honey and some green grape jelly in the pantry," she told her. "Help yourself."

Margaret Hobart looked soft and helpless. "I don't know how," she said. "At home the servant does those things." She settled herself in her chair.

"You remind me of your ma," said Miz Liz.

"Oh, thank you!" said Margaret Hobart. She batted her eyes again.

"Didn't mean it that way," said Miz Liz. "Got something in your eye? There's some wash soap in the laundry."

Margaret Hobart looked at her, and her face began to get red and her eyes opened wide.

"There's nothing in my eye and I don't want any of your old grape jelly and I think I'm going to have a tantrum!" Then she choked and then she began to howl.

My Uncle Henry came in right then. He was dressed in his office clothes, but he had his double-barreled shotgun in his hand. I knew he'd been having it checked at the gunsmith's. He looked at Margaret Hobart, and then he looked at Miz Liz and me.

"A Kentucky gentleman cannot strike a lady," he said, "but there are ways around these things." He handed me his big shotgun. "Better use the choke. It doesn't make as much noise, and the shot doesn't scatter so much."

By the time I'd looked to see if the gun was loaded, Margaret Hobart wasn't there any more. She'd run out the way she'd come, but we could hear her screaming, "I hate all of you and when I tell my mother she'll hate you too, and when my father comes home, if he ever does, he'll shoot *you*!"

Uncle Henry sat down. "I'll have some chicken too, Miz Liz. Been carving people up all day, and it's hungry work."

2

I HAVE A BROTHER, BUT HE'S A LOT OLDER AND I haven't seen him for a couple of years. He's in Europe, and I think that's a good place for him. As soon as he got out of the University of Virginia (they have the biggest boxwood in Charlottesville I ever saw anywhere) he went off to look for himself. He thinks he's pretty good, but I don't, and my Uncle Henry doesn't like him. He never said so, but I know. My brother has a girl to help him locate his identity, the way they say, but she's from Chattanooga and is as bad as he is.

My father is tall and thin and sort of stooped and squints like anything when he takes off his eyeglasses. He's the librarian at the college, and I guess he's a professor too because people call him Fess and say, "Good morning, Fess" when they see him if it's morning, but he doesn't care what they call him. Half the time he doesn't even see them. What he does is think about books all the time.

He has a couple of thousand books or maybe three. Some of them were my great-grandfather's and some were my grandfather's, and they are bound in leather or what my father calls Spanish calf or half morocco and things like that, and they are old and they smell old. The library in our house is lined to the ceiling with them. There's a ladder there, and you need it to reach some of them.

Most of the books are first editions or what my father calls "association copies" or have the authors' names in them that they wrote themselves. My father lives in his library when he's home. He sits behind a great big desk that was my grandfather's and is covered with booksellers catalogues and things like that. He has about all the books there are, but he keeps getting more either for himself or for the college. At the prices he pays he could get big brand-new books with pictures in them, but he doesn't want those.

In the trunk of his car he keeps cartons and burlap sacks so that when he goes to sales in Atlanta or New York or Philadelphia he can bring back even more books. On his desk he has a black telephone with a trigger underneath that says "off" and "on." He keeps it on "off" so he can call out when he wants to but hardly ever does, but nobody can call him. That is, they can call but he doesn't answer.

Once I asked him why he became a librarian. He said it was because he didn't want to be a lion tamer. He says things like that. Once when my uncle was trying to get him to go fishing with us he said he couldn't because the early bookworm catches the bird. Another time he would not go with my mother to meet some people because he said they were probably dead. He says the only live people he knows are in the books in his library.

So my mother had to go with some of my aunts and uncles who don't matter. My mother doesn't care anything about books. She runs things.

My mother is a Social and Civic Leader. That's what it always says in the newspapers. "The Social and Civic Leader Sybil Trewbridge . . ." it says. She has a fancy gold French telephone in her room, and if it has an "off" switch, she never uses it. She runs the D.A.R. and the Daughters of the Confederacy, and the Historical Association, and the charities, and all kinds of committees and movements. She talks into the gold telephone all the time, even in the mornings when she stays in her bed, which is a big four-poster. I guess she sleeps in it at night but it is really sort of her office. She telephones from it or dictates speeches into the tape recorder on a little stand that rolls on casters so she can pull it close to her bedside.

Uncle Henry says she is like Mark Twain. He used to work in bed like that and smoke cigars while he was doing it. My mother does not smoke cigars, at least I never saw her do it. Probably she doesn't have time or can't find one because the big bed is always covered with letters and papers and programs, and she waves you away while she's talking on the telephone if you go in there, so I never do.

I have a green telephone in my room, which is a long way from theirs. They said I had to have one so I chose green. The reason I have to have one is because my father said we had to have some way to keep in touch. As he never answers his and my mother is always talking to hers his idea doesn't work, and I knew it wouldn't, but I didn't say anything because all I wanted to do was move. It was because of Cicero. Even Miz Liz said I couldn't keep a dog in my room upstairs, even if Cicero is only a beagle, so I moved out of my bedroom into a big room off the back kitchen. There are a lot of rooms between that we don't use except at Christmas or commencement or some other time when we have lots of house guests. Most of the time the things in them are covered with white dustcloths. My room is a good room, cool in summer and warm in winter, and I can keep all my things there.

Some fellows let their dogs sleep with them. I wouldn't do that. Dogs are sensitive, and they can catch cold or pneumonia from you. What I did was make bunk beds like they have in a caboose out of two strong cots I found in the attic. Miz Liz helped me. Cicero sleeps in the lower berth, and I sleep over him. That's best for him and for me too. It keeps me from getting dog fleas. Every fall I get sand fleas down by the branch and get itchy welts till they get used to me, so I don't need dog fleas any time.

It's good in my room. I took the old wallpaper off, and it has plank walls that are well chinked. Cicero and I have our own television, and we watch it sometimes, but mostly I just turn on the radio for company, and Cicero watches me clean and oil my .22 if we've been out that day or mess with my arrowheads and other things or do my homework, when I do it.

Usually I eat with Miz Liz in the kitchen and I like that, but when we have company or when Miz Liz says we have to act civilized sometimes, we eat in the big dining room. The lamps throw gleaming light on the old mahogany table, but the oil portraits in their heavy gold frames are in shadow on the wall. My mother tells my father where she was that day or where she is going the next, and my father says a dealer in Chicago has a first edition of *The Tatler,* five volumes in the original calf or something like that, and I just eat.

There's always plenty, and it's good and hot with hot biscuits or hush puppies, so I don't mind, but I like the kitchen better. No one keeps asking me questions, and I can help myself if I want more, and no one says kale is good for growing boys or gets asking if I've been eating chili again.

I know a place downtown where you can get a big bowl of really hot chili and a plate of French fries for sixty-five cents. I go there a lot. I've eaten so much chili I'm probably part Mexican, but the French fries are American even if they call them French so I guess it balances out.

I have a system too. If I want something or think I'd better get permission for something, I wait till I know my father is in his library. He is always polite and looks up from what he is doing and takes off his glasses and squints to show he is listening to me. I ask him fast, and he is so anxious to get his glasses back on so he can see that he almost always says yes. Then he looks surprised to see I am there, and I say, "Thank you, Father," and get away before he can change his mind. Sometimes I think he has had so much trouble trying to help my brother who is looking for his identity that anything I do is a relief, but sometimes I think he forgets about me and wonders who I am and is a little shocked when he sees me.

I work it differently with my mother. It's pretty hard to see her except by accident on the stairs or in the hall or when we all have dinner together. When she is not talking to her French telephone she is at a luncheon or a tea or a club meeting or being a chairwoman. My green telephone really comes in handy then. I pick it up to make sure she is talking to someone and then ask her or tell her. She knows the person she is talking to thinks I am in the same room and says, "Of course, dear. Aren't children delightful? So imaginative!"

One day when it was raining and I didn't have anything else to do I called and asked her if Cicero and I could go to the North Pole after school. She was talking to the rector that time so she said, "Of course, dear. Be sure to wear your rubbers, and you won't forget to say your little prayers, will you, dear." Cicero looked at me sideways when he heard her and showed the whites of his eyes. One of them has red lines in it where a cat scratched him.

My Uncle Henry is as tall as my father and sort of looks like him except that he isn't stooped and doesn't squint and walks with long, loose steps. He dresses differently at different times. When he goes to his office in the Medical Center downtown or to the hospital or the clinic he wears a dark suit and a white shirt with a bow tie. He told me he wears bow ties because the other kind dangle and get tangled with his stethoscope or into a patient's mouth if he is in bed.

Half the time though he wears khaki chinos or corduroys tucked into leather boots and a flannel shirt and a hunting coat and drives his Land Rover, which is like a Jeep only the spare tire is on the hood. In the back he has his 12 gauge or his fly rod or his casting rod and a sack of oats or a piece of farm machinery he's taking to or from the blacksmith shop. Uncle Henry has a four-hundred acre farm about four miles out, and what a farm! Rolling fields, bluegrass pasture, woods, raccoons, opossums, hedgehogs, fox squirrels. He has a man and his wife out there and they look after the cows and horses and raise his black burley tobacco and watermelons and feed the hogs and Uncle Henry and me when I'm along, which is as often as I can make it. I love that farm. When my grandfather died, my father took our house, and my Uncle Henry took the farm.

The sky is a cornflower blue out there except at dusk and then it is almost purple like tumbleweed. The doves fly over in fall. There are quail in the brush. Most years I see a deer. Once it was a doe and a little fawn; another time, a big buck with eight-point antlers. They come at night to the old apple orchard. Just once my uncle and I saw a brown bear drinking at the branch. We could have shot him easily for he just stood and looked at us, but Uncle Henry shook his head, and I didn't want to either. "Good luck, bear!" my uncle called, and the bear walked away on his hind feet, still looking back at us.

If people call my father Fess, they call my uncle Doc or Doctor Trewbridge or Henry or Hank or Major, which is what he was in the war. It depends on who they are and how they know him. Uncle Henry never seems to know who he is or what he looks like or what he is doing. He just is it and does it and does it fast and sure and laughs or smiles or scowls because he wants to laugh or smile or scowl, not because he thinks someone expects him to.

Uncle Henry has a room at our house with some of his clothes in it. He sleeps in it when he is out very late or when he has to operate early in the morning or has to catch a plane.

"I love this old house," he told me once. "Like your father, I was born in it, though he beat me to it. Perhaps I'll die in it, but not until I've lived. I'm working hard and that's living; and I'm not working hard and that's living too."

One night at dinner my mother said, "Henry, dear, if you'd only marry and settle down."

My uncle laughed at her and my mother got angry. She always does when anyone laughs at her.

"That last girl — hasn't there been scandal enough in this family?"

"Sybil!" said my father. He doesn't usually speak that sharply.

"Vergil, drink your soup and take your elbow off the table!" my mother said to me to get even, and Uncle Henry laughed again.

People like to see my uncle when he strides down the street or they get out of his way. He can go anywhere he wants any time he wants to. He can go up into the mountains anywhere and people won't even shoot at him. Some of the men touch their black felt hats to him. They all look at him and don't say anything. You know how they are in the mountains when they like you and trust you.

Uncle Henry takes care of them. Once a week he goes up those steep dirt roads in the Rover and patches them up if they have a cold or a broken arm or something. Once he took a cal. .30 slug out of one of them when he got shot out hunting, and once he helped them get a cow out of a sink hole. He got a sling under it and hoisted it with a little derrick from the farm and then set its shoulder and kept it off the ground in another sling for over a week. He's as good as any vet.

Two boys in the mountains are named after him because he delivered them. Know what he charges up in the mountains? Nothing. Sometimes, though, he finds a gallon of homemade whiskey in the back of his car or a fat opossum or a bushel of mountain apples. He likes the mountain people and they like him.

3

"I'M STUCK," SAID MARGARET HOBART. "I'M HARDLY ever stuck, but this time I am and you have to help me." She sounded all bothered and coaxing.

I was feeling pretty good after a big bowl of chili, and things had been going pretty smoothly for a while. Margaret Hobart hadn't seemed so bad lately, and I didn't want any fuss, so I made a mistake. I said I would.

"It's for my Special Project report in school," she said. "Last time I took a piece of mama's antique needlepoint and showed it to them and told them about it. The time before I wore one of Great-Grandmama's crinolines — I looked beautiful in it too. I explained how clothes change over the centuries and why. I always get an "A" but this time I want to do something modern."

"I don't have anything modern," I said. "Everything I have is old."

Margaret Hobart looked at me hard. She sort of inspected me.

"Stop that," I said.

"Stop what?"

"Stop looking at me."

"I like to look at you," she said. "Everybody does."

I was beginning to get suspicious so I didn't say anything.

"I have my talk all written out," she said.

"You can't have Cicero or my .22 or the 20 gauge Uncle Henry gave me for my birthday or my bass rod or my bike, and those are about all I have."

"I don't want any of your nasty old things!"

"Cicero isn't a nasty old thing. He's only three, and he's pedigreed."

"I just want you," said Margaret Hobart the way the heroine does in the love stories on television.

"Me!"

"I'll say you are my cousin and then go on and explain why there are families and about family relationships and the need for understanding in the family and broken homes and all that. That's all the teachers talk about."

"No!"

"You have to be with it now, and what's more with it than the family? You'll be the center of attention."

"I don't want to be the center of anything."

"Ruth King and June Wyatt are in my class. They'll be green with envy. They envy me anyway because I'm your cousin."

"They do?"

"And it's Friday afternoon. You'll get out of your math class."

I remembered then that we were going to have a math test Friday. Margaret Hobart didn't know that. I thought about it. "Well, maybe."

"I *knew* you'd help me. You're always helping me, aren't you? You wouldn't even shoot me when you had the chance."

I should have known then that Margaret Hobart was up to no good. She never forgets but always schemes even after you have forgotten what she is getting even for. The trouble is I was thinking about that math test.

"I didn't say I would for sure."

"Yes, you did, and you can't go back on a promise!"

"Oh, all right then."

For two days I wished I hadn't said it. The way you can get into things without meaning to! Every time she saw me Margaret Hobart gave me the new smile she's been trying, widening her eyes, showing all her teeth, and tipping her head to the side a little.

I decided to get sick and stay home from school Friday. I don't like to fake things so I ate six hard green apples from an old tree near the house, and I waded in the branch and got my feet wet, and I put my hands in poison ivy. Nothing worked.

I didn't say anything about it to Miz Liz. I knew my mother and father wouldn't care as long as I didn't bother them, and I hadn't seen Uncle Henry in a couple of weeks. In our room the night before I asked Cicero what he thought I should do, but he just yawned and scratched himself, which is what he usually does. When I said, "Oh, you're no good and never were!" he tried to wag his tail but couldn't because he had a burr caught in it. I had to get my knife and cut it out of his hair.

The next morning I put on my oldest clothes and didn't brush and comb my hair. Margaret Hobart wasn't going to make a fool of me! During the morning I began to sweat, and I didn't want my lunch. Then Margaret Hobart, who was all dressed up, came for me. My teacher had already given her permission. She smiled at me as if I were as cute as a gold-fish, which is what I felt like.

The first couple of minutes in front of Margaret Hobart's class were pretty bad. My feet and hands were cold. My face was burning, and my brain was numb. I could hardly see the class because my eyes were blurred. The class was quiet at first but when the teacher told them that Margaret Hobart had brought me to help on her project report they burst out laughing. I wanted to disappear.

Then Margaret Hobart came up and stood next to me, and as soon as she spoke I knew she had trapped me.

"This is a child, a boy child," she said. "It is a typical specimen of the male young. It is crummy, but they all are."

That did it. Margaret Hobart had got me and she'd done it

on purpose. I wished I were back taking the math test, but that was only for a couple of seconds. Margaret Hobart gave me that grown-up smile again as if she were amused at what I looked like. The class laughed even more loudly.

I'm pretty peaceable; I really am, but when I get angry I don't get all hot and bothered. I get cold and I turn pale. I kind of steady down. My eyes cleared and my stomach felt as if it were there again. I looked hard at Margaret Hobart's class, and some of them stopped laughing. I know most of the fellows in it, and they know me. I'm taller than some of them even if they are two years ahead of me, and they know what I can do to them if I want to. I didn't care about the girls except Ruth. She has big blue eyes and she was looking straight at me and not laughing, as if she were on my side.

"Because it is sort of human a little boy can stand upright on his hind feet," said Margaret Hobart. "Stand for the boys and girls, Vergil."

The class was very quiet now. They wanted to see what would happen. I stared at Margaret Hobart stupidly as if I didn't understand.

She acted as if she were being patient with an idiot. She looked at the teacher to show they were the only real adults among amusing children.

"Stand up on your hind feet, Vergil," she said kindly. "Stand up and beg."

I thought about it for a minute. Then I got down on all fours.

A couple of girls giggled, and the teacher tried not to smile. The rest were all watching and waiting.

Margaret Hobart looked a little upset, but she went on with her speech. "When I go to Sweetbriar College in Virginia, which, of course, is the best, I will study all about people in physiology so — "

"She means psychology," I told the class. My uncle had explained the difference to me.

Margaret Hobart began to turn red. "A little boy can talk,"

she said, "because it has a tongue like people, only smaller."

I made my tongue as large as I could when I stuck it out. Then I barked. Then I howled like Cicero when he is after a rabbit or a fox.

"Stop it, Vergil!" cried Margaret Hobart.

I cowered away as if she had struck me. I've learned a lot from Cicero.

"Stop that!" said Margaret Hobart. "Miss Kinningworth, make him stop!"

"Now, Margaret Hobart, we mustn't lose our temper," said Miss Kinningworth.

I pretended to brush back my hair with my right hand but in doing it I somehow thumbed my nose at Margaret Hobart. The teacher didn't see it, but the class did and so did Margaret Hobart.

"Small boys," she shouted, "grow up to be men just as girls grow up to be young women like me. Girls become graceful, but boys don't. Their voices change, and they get even awkwarder."

She looked at me as if she'd won and had got even now. I looked back at her but didn't say anything. That upset her again, and she lost her place in her notes and dropped two pages and one went under the teacher's desk. She scrambled after it and got her hands all dirty and a smudge on her nose. The class was really laughing now but not at me, at her.

I decided to help her.

"Boys do have feet," I said. "They use them to stand on and walk on and sometimes they kick people."

Margaret Hobart was just getting up and made a good target. I made a gesture with my right foot, and the class cheered, even the girls.

"They have legs too," I said. "They bend at joints which are called knees." I showed them. "Their arms bend at other joints which are called elbows." I shook my fist at Jamie

Hector who was looking smart and he looked scared instead.

"A boy child like the specimen we have here!" screamed Margaret Hobart — she had to scream to make herself heard — "a specimen like this one, is a problem to his parents but they love him because it is the nature of people to love their young no matter what they are like." She sounded very learned.

"It's the nature of dogs and bears too," I said as if I had just thought of something wonderful.

"You be still!" screamed Margaret Hobart. "You keep quiet! You — you shut up!"

"Now, Margaret Hobart," said Miss Kinningworth so quietly that the class knew she meant it and was quiet too, "we mustn't get carried away, must we."

"I'll carry *him* away! I'll *kill* him and *then* I'll carry him away!"

She made a dive for me, but I dodged behind the teacher's desk, and Miss Kinningworth jumped up to protect me, and most of the class jumped up and yelled.

"Thank you, Margaret Hobart," the teacher shouted. "This has been most interesting, and I'm sure we have all learned a great deal from it. Thank you too, Vergil."

Margaret Hobart wasn't listening. She was jumping up and down and howling. Even the boys drew back as she burst out with, "I'm so *mad* I'm mad at everybody there *is* and I wish there were more people in the world so I could be mad at them too — but not people like *you all*!" Then she burst into tears and then she burst out of the room.

That's a lot of bursting but she did it. Margaret Hobart is good at it.

4

I FELT PRETTY GOOD AT FIRST, BUT THEN I GOT feeling sorry for Margaret Hobart because that's the way I am. I knew she'd tell her mother too, and her mother would tell my mother. Then my mother would telephone the rector and the teacher and the principal and the guidance counselor and the Daughters of the Confederacy and say she had done her best with me, heaven knows, and she did not know what more she could do and would they please help her.

She'd insist my father speak to me, and he would take off his glasses and squint and not listen and say he was sure I didn't plan to do it again. Then he'd put his glasses back on and ask me what it was I did anyway. After I'd told him he'd take them off to show I had his full attention and say, "You know you mustn't upset your mother, don't you?"

Once I asked him why not, and he smiled and nodded and said, "That's a good boy."

That's the way it always goes, and that's why I say cousins are worse than the measles.

I was pretty down by the time I reached home, but I needn't have been. Miz Liz was waiting for me.

"Where you been? You have to hurry. Your uncle called, and you're going to spend the weekend out to the farm with him. He's coming by for you right off. I packed your bag but you better get another sweater or your leather jacket because it can get cold nights now, and take your boots if you're going to go sloshing around in the fields."

I ran for them and my .22 and grabbed the bag and by that time Uncle Henry's Rover was in the drive. I said goodbye to Miz Liz and ran out.

Uncle Henry was still in his city clothes but nothing else in his farm car was. He had a couple of bags of feed and his 12 gauge and boxes of shells for it and for my 20 gauge, which I keep out at the farm.

"Doves flying," he said when he saw me look at the things. "Abner told me. We might get a few — but not if you take all day."

I didn't take two seconds to jump in beside him, and he shifted gears and we went off fast.

The thing I like best about the farm is just being there. When you're at my uncle's farm there isn't any other place anywhere, and you don't want there to be. It's big and broad, and if you look over the fields, the sky seems to come down to meet them as if they belonged together.

It's an honest farm too, a working farm. Uncle Henry says a farm isn't honest unless it pays for its keep, and his does. He raises black burley tobacco and lespedeza and corn for feed crops. He has a herd of Holsteins with a few Jerseys to keep up the butter fat and a lot of hogs. They get the skimmed milk from the separator.

The farm house is big and solid, but that's about all it is. It's sort of shabby. Uncle Henry says you take care of your land and your barns and your stock and your fences but, as long as it doesn't fall down, the house doesn't matter that much. You can always tell a good farm. It's one where the outbuildings look better than the farmhouse.

Almost before the car stopped I jumped out and ran to the paddock to see Scalpel and Stethoscope. The paddock has a white rail fence like the big horse farms around Lexington and Paris, and it has an exercise track but it's small. I painted most of the fence myself.

Scalpel is just my uncle's hunter. He is a big bay and all right, but Stethoscope is different. My uncle bought him at the yearling sale in Lexington so he's a Thoroughbred. My uncle didn't go to the sale to buy a colt, and he didn't want a racehorse, but he saw Stethoscope. He had a sore throat. My uncle could tell by the way he kept twisting his neck, and he had a muscle pull in his leg. The breeders had probably just brought him along with their show yearlings because he was there and they had room in the truck. He looked at my uncle and my uncle looked at him, and they liked each other, and Uncle Henry knew he could fix him up. Nobody else wanted him so he bought him pretty cheap.

Stethoscope saw me almost as soon as I saw him and galloped up to the fence and almost into it before he braked. Then he rolled his eyes and stamped his right forefoot with the white stocking on it and pushed his head over the rail and nuzzled me when I reached out to him.

At home I'm just Vergil Trewbridge and I'm just Verge Trewbridge at school, but at the farm I'm somebody and Stethoscope knows it. I'm not just his exercise boy but his best friend.

My uncle had followed me, and Scalpel, who doesn't bother much with Stethoscope except to nip at him if he gets in his way, walked over slowly to see him and sniff at him. Scalpel is dignified and doesn't show everything he feels. He's a Thoroughbred too. He can go like anything, and I think he could jump over the moon like the cow in the nursery rhyme if he really wanted to, but when he doesn't want to, he keeps his speed and power to himself.

Uncle Henry stroked his silky neck and told him he was a no-account spookendyke and not worth his feed, and Scalpel listened and poked his head at my uncle's coat.

I saw something. "He's like you," I said to Uncle Henry.

"Of course, he is. Any animal gets to be like the people he's with. Mean people have mean dogs; good dogs belong to good people. See a vicious horse or dog and you know the kind of people he spends his time with."

I kept petting Stethoscope, who isn't really full grown yet, and he began to duck his head up and down at me the way he does when he's happy.

Scalpel kept nudging my uncle. "He likes you," I said.

My uncle laughed. "He doesn't love me. He loves my tobacco, and he can smell it." Uncle Henry poured some out of his pouch into his hand and Scalpel licked it up. Then he begged for more.

I know that tobacco. It's our own black burley, and there are hands of it hanging in the big barn. It's strong enough to take the top of your head off. I know because I've tried it. Uncle Henry smokes it all the time; sometimes he chews a little when he's in the barn and doesn't want to light his pipe because of the hay. Some of the burley is mine. I have a quarter acre that I plant and take care of myself. That's where most of my income comes from because Uncle Henry gives me my share when he sells the crop.

Stethoscope got tired of me. He wheeled and trotted off, then stood in the middle of the paddock looking back at us. That's one of the things he does. For a colt, Stethoscope thinks a lot. Sometimes he just dozes in the sun and tips over a little while he sleeps. Sometimes when he's out in the pasture he races himself or decides to fight the wind and dives into it with his teeth bared and his mane flying. He loves that.

Uncle Henry was looking up at the sky. "There's some flying over now. See — over the south field coming out of the woods. Better hurry!"

In the house we changed fast into woods clothes and our boots. Then we started out through the high grass, turning purple for fall, toward the branch and the woods. I had the 20 gauge, and my uncle had his 12 gauge under his arm and was holding Dave on a leash.

I have to be careful when I bring Cicero out to the farm. There are two dogs there, and they think he is a young nuisance. Dan is a shepherd and a working dog. He drives the cows. It annoys him when Cicero wants to play. Dave is a hunting dog, a pointer. He knows his business and doesn't want Cicero getting in his way.

It wasn't warm and it wasn't cold out in the fields but just right. The sun was getting low and the sky was right clear. All the smells of fall were all around us. My uncle and I walked together for a while, but then we separated, and the silence a long way from the house was deep. I came to the woods and the first thing I saw was a red squirrel. He saw me too and dodged around the trunk of an oak about thirty feet from the ground. I wished I'd brought my .22. I wouldn't waste a shotgun shell on a squirrel.

I walked a long way almost forgetting what we had come for. Then I heard my uncle's gun, both barrels, and knew he had got some doves. Of course, he had the dog and I didn't, but with doves you don't really need a dog. They're pretty stupid and fly in a bunch in a pretty straight line.

Then some birds came right at me over the trees. I shot too fast and didn't lead enough so I missed. Maybe I didn't even want to hit them. I don't think I did, but I wanted my uncle to hear I was attending to business. I heard his gun again, just once this time, and knew he'd got more doves. I reloaded and kept on going.

Margaret Hobart had tried to get even with me and got fooled, but I didn't feel so good either. Shows what comes of things like oral reports. Some people like to tell people things. They think it shows how smart they are. I never tell anybody anything unless it's someone I like a lot; I don't ask people questions if I can help it except the way to some place or something like that. They're sure to tell you more than you want to hear anyway.

I hadn't meant to think of Margaret Hobart and school so I stopped. I heard more shots, looked up, and saw that Uncle Henry was driving a flock of birds my way. There were a lot of them and they were moving fast. Almost without thinking I

24

brought down two. That was enough to show my uncle I could.

Then Dave came rushing through the grass and up to me and licked my hand. My uncle came along after him. As he topped a rise I saw him against the sky and he looked dark and big.

He looked at my bag. "Only two?"

"I muffed it once."

"Happens. I've twelve. There's still light. We'll get a few more."

We walked along together but about twenty feet apart. Dave scouted ahead.

"Why doesn't my father ever do anything like this?"

My uncle didn't look at me because he was watching the sky, but he answered. "He used to. Your father is a good shot."

"He is?"

"And he rides better than I. He could teach you a few tricks."

"He could! Then what happened?"

We kept walking a safe distance apart but my uncle looked over at me this time.

"I think it began when Mother — your grandmother — taught him to read and write. He could read before he went to school, and he never got over it — then there were a few other things."

I didn't ask what the things were because I was watching the sky too. A big flock, black against the remaining light, was coming toward us as if the birds were hurrying to get somewhere before dark. Uncle and I waited. We shot at almost the same time and birds fell. Dave raced to retrieve and uncle stuffed them into the big bag pocket at the back of his tan hunting coat.

"That's more like it," he said. "Let's go home. No point in being greedy."

You could already see the sliver of a moon and the bright

evening star. We'd come a long way and had a long way back. It was getting cool, but the country was just as good in twilight as in the day because it's always good. For a long time we didn't say anything. Then I began to think of Margaret Hobart again. First she'd said she was going to talk about families in her project.

"Are broken homes really that bad?" I asked my uncle.

He had stopped to light his pipe. He got it going and laughed. "Been breaking yours?"

"No," I said. "I don't think ours was ever put together."

He was just putting his pipe back in his mouth but he stopped. I could not see all his face because it was getting dark fast now, but I knew he was looking at me because I could see his teeth, which are white and strong looking.

"Out of the mouths of babes!" he said.

I know that line from the Bible so I said, "I'm not a babe, and I'm not a suckling either. Sucklings are hogs."

We were getting near the house and passing the orchard. Uncle Henry picked an apple off a tree and stuck it in my mouth. "See what you feel like now," he said.

I took the apple out of my mouth and laughed and then I ate it. It was a good sweet firm apple, not mushy like a MacIntosh, which some people who don't know think are good apples.

Mrs. Kinney had a big dinner ready for us when we got cleaned up. Mr. Kinney is my uncle's farmer, and they live there all the time. We had roast pork and chitlins and yams and greens and cider. One of the farmers Mr. Kinney knows back in the hills has a press, and this was some of the first that year. It was sweet cider though that farmer makes mostly hard cider and applejack. Mrs. Kinney kept filling my plate and I kept eating and eating.

I was so full of food and fresh air that I went to bed early while my uncle and Mr. Kinney, who is little and brown and wrinkled and has white hair, were talking farm things in my uncle's room that is full of guns and books and pictures. He has a lot of books, not just medical books, but not as many as my father.

My room at the farm is kind of bare like most of the rooms there, but it's only for sleeping in. The sheets were cold at first, and it was black dark. I wanted to light a match to see if I was still there, but I didn't. I wondered if Cicero was all right, and that's the last thing I remember.

It was a pretty day in the morning. I saw that right away. It was early, but I could hear sounds in the house so I knew the others were up. I don't like to lie abed so I hurried to wash and dress.

It wasn't until I got to the kitchen that I found out from Mrs. Kinney that my uncle had been called into the hospital to perform an emergency operation in the middle of the night. He would not be back until late afternoon. That's happened before. Mr. Kinney was out at the barn doing the chores. I knew that because I could hear the milking machines and the separator. I heard the hogs squealing as he took them pails of milk. They'll be butchering soon. I don't want to be around for that.

I didn't know I was hungry again but I was. I don't know how many hot cakes I ate with blackstrap molasses. I talked to Mrs. Kinney a while. Then I took my .22 and went out front.

The farmhouse is way back from the road, and the big lawn is always close-cropped because my uncle keeps a couple of sheep for lawn mowers. They were out there now and working hard. Each side of the walk to the house there is a holly about forty feet tall. One is a male and one is a female. That is the one the squirrels get after because it has berries. They were turning red now, and the squirrels cut the twigs clean as with an axe to get them, just the way they chisel oak branches for acorns. They can have the acorns, but I like holly.

I took a place in the shadow of the house about fifty feet away. Almost right away I saw a squirrel. I aimed and squeezed carefully but just as I got off the shot he flicked away. Three squirrels jumped out of the holly and ran as fast as they could. I just sat on the ground out of sight and waited. The sun was warming the earth and lighting the fields. I looked at everything but did not move. You can't if you are hunting, and squirrels are smart.

I saw one come back but I still didn't move. I let him climb well into the tree. I could still see him through the branches and the leaves. When he was all set, I was too. I squeezed off another shot and he dropped flat to the ground. I'd got rid of one of them anyway.

I was sorry my uncle had been called back to work because he doesn't get much free time, but I don't mind being by myself when I have something to do. I like to do things I can do alone because that is the way you are most of the time. In school the teachers call this "antisocial," and one of them wrote on my report card that I am antisocial, and maybe I am but that doesn't change what I said.

I've noticed that people who really do anything do it by themselves. My father fusses with his books and papers and whatever else it is he does by himself. My uncle isn't being social when he is taking out an appendix or a gall bladder or putting in a plastic artery the way he had to do for Mr. Baker. He doesn't call a meeting or form an association or go on a march with a lot of other people; he does it by himself. Then he's responsible to himself and nobody else the way I am to me. Daniel Boone didn't hunt and fish and trap with a crowd. He went alone.

My mother, of course, never does anything by herself. She does it with everybody she can reach over her gold telephone, and she can reach plenty of people. Mr. Kinney doesn't do the milking all by himself. The cows have to be there too, but that's different.

I stayed out front most of the morning, and I got three squirrels. I gave them to Mrs. Kinney because the Kinneys are back country folk who came from there and like squirrels and opossum pie. I never wanted to try either one myself.

My uncle didn't come back till late that day, and he wasn't saying much. That night we ate the doves, and Mr. Kinney said they were wonderful. There isn't much to them but thin bones but I didn't say anything because you are supposed to like them.

"Squab on toast is a delicacy in fine restaurants," my uncle said, "and this is about the same but better." I think he said it just to say something. He saw me looking at him and shook his head just a little so that no one else would notice. Afterward he told me. "I lost the patient. You do sometimes. You'd think I'd get used to it."

I kept hoping it wouldn't, but Monday morning came. My uncle had to be at the hospital early so the sun wasn't really up when we left the farm. I got home even before Miz Liz was up. After breakfast I got away from the house as soon as I could.

5

CICERO WAS WAITING FOR ME WHEN I CAME OUT OF school. Either he wants to go to school or wishes I didn't for he often comes. I don't know how long he had been waiting, but he was right glad to see me and wagged himself all over me and slobbered.

"Oh, stop it!" I said.

He stopped waggling and wriggling right off and dropped his ears and lay down on his stomach. I had to pet him and hug him hard before he felt all right again and ran off barking in front of me. I'm always having to make up to people when I haven't done anything to them. I really hadn't done anything to Margaret Hobart either, but I still wished I didn't have to go home.

I let the school bus go the way I do half the time. It's about a mile and a half home but Cicero was with me and I wasn't in any hurry anyway. First we went and got a bowl of chili, but Cicero wouldn't eat any.

When I got home I started for the front steps but stopped when I heard women's voices coming from the living room. I knew whose voices they were too. I sneaked around back and slipped through from the kitchen to where I could hear from a dark place in the hall. Before I could stop him Cicero came too. I had to hold his muzzle so he wouldn't make any noise.

"So I thought you should know immediately what we have decided to do," said Margaret Hobart's mother. I have to call her "aunt," but she's really only a far-off cousin of my father's. "We are sending Margaret Hobart to my sister in

Richmond for a long, long visit. She will go to a very select girls' school there."

"I see," said my mother as if she were thinking of something else. I could not see her from where Cicero and I were hiding.

"After Vergil humiliated her before all her friends she could hardly return to school here."

No one else spoke.

"Actually we have been considering this step for a long time. This is not the environment in which to bring up a sensitive and delicate young girl."

Miz Liz spoke so slowly and distinctly I knew she was angry. "Can't say as I know any place that is, not when the girl is sensitive and delicate the way your young one is."

"I think I hear the kettle boiling, Elizabeth," said my mother quickly.

I didn't hear it and I was nearer the kitchen than they were, but I wasn't listening for kettles. I just had time to shrink back against the wall before Miz Liz pushed by. She walks kind of stiff and has to look where she's going.

"You don't know what it is to have a daughter who is an only child," said Margaret Hobart's mother in a kind of faint voice.

My mother didn't like this so she said, "I think it is unfortunate to have just one child." Her voice was harder and clearer than it usually is.

I guess my aunt didn't hear her because she said, "Especially such a lovely young woman as Margaret Hobart is getting to be."

"I haven't seen the child for some time," said my mother. This is true because she's usually in her room or out somewhere when Margaret Hobart is around, or even when she isn't. "I'm sure she takes after you."

Margaret Hobart's mother is a little fat and lately she's been a blonde. I could see her through the open door. She opened her eyes wide, and they are big and soft and brown like the cows have at the farm. "I was campus queen at Homecoming, you know."

"Yes, I know. At George Peabody Teachers College, wasn't it?" My mother went to Ward Belmont, which is in Nashville too, and I don't think the two places like each other much. "You were only a junior too, weren't you?"

"Yes, dear," said my aunt proudly. She tried to look modest.

"It must be wonderful to look back," said my mother. "Of course, my life is so full I seldom have time to look back that far. Really I don't know how I manage to do all I do. Just the other day Greta Harvey said to me, 'Sybil Trewbridge, how *do* you manage to do it all?'"

"She should ask me," said Miz Liz, coming in with the silver teapot and sugar and creamer on an old black tray. She put it down hard on one of the little tables.

"Really, Elizabeth, must we always use that horrid tray. Any of the silver ones would be much better."

"All need polishin'. Leave the boy be," she said flatly.

Margaret Hobart's mother gasped. "Well, I never!"

"I'll pour," said my mother quickly. "Lemon or sugar?"

"I don't think I care for any tea, thank you," said my aunt, getting up. "I must go. My husband will be home any time now."

"Not if he can help it he won't," said Miz Liz.

"I didn't come here to be spoken to in this way! I came to tell you how horribly Vergil treated Margaret Hobart and find out what you intend to do about it."

"Vergil is a boy and Margaret Hobart is a girl," said my mother as if that settled the matter.

It was the first time I ever heard my mother stand up for me. I was surprised. I knew right away though that it was just because she doesn't really like Margaret Hobart's mother. I picked up Cicero so he wouldn't make any noise and went away without making any myself. Before we got to our room we heard the front door close hard.

A minute later Miz Liz came for me. "Come for your milk and sandwich," she said, "though why I should make sandwiches for a body stands listening and looking where he shouldn't be looking and listening I don't know."

I ate the sandwich and drank the milk and then I went to our room and lay down on Cicero's bed. I didn't feel like climbing up to my own. I just lay there and looked out at the sky. I didn't want to do anything. I knew I didn't have to but I still felt a little guilty about Margaret Hobart even if it was all her fault. Cicero stuck his cold nose into my neck to see what was the matter with me, and I jumped, but then I stroked him, and he was warm and this time I let him lie down next to me. It was his bed.

"Verge!"

It was a whisper and so low I thought I'd just imagined it and didn't move.

"Verge, may I come in?" The door opened slowly. It was Margaret Hobart and she was almost out of breath. Cicero wagged his tail at her, but he didn't move so I couldn't get up.

I didn't say anything but Margaret Hobart did.

"Mother thinks I am in my room, but I slipped out the back and ran across the field. I just had to come and thank you before I go."

"Thank me?" I pushed Cicero off onto the floor, which he didn't like, and got up.

"Of course. I've been wanting to go to Richmond all along, and I might never have made it without your help."

"You're not mad at me?"

"Mad at you for getting me just what I want? I have a lovely room at my aunt's. All the girls from the best families in Virginia go to the school. I'll have ballet lessons and everything. Who wants to stay in this old backwoods? I'll be all grown up when I come back — I am now really but people are so stupid."

Margaret Hobart's eyes were shining and she looked all

excited, but she was still whispering because she didn't want anyone else in the house to hear, and I whispered because she did.

"I'm glad you're not mad at me," I said, and I really meant it.

"I was just pretending at school," said Margaret Hobart. "I fooled all of you, didn't I? Probably I'll be an actress. I hope you won't miss me too much. I'll be home for Christmas vacation."

"I won't miss you," I said.

"Yes, you will," said Margaret Hobart, and before I could stop her she kissed me hard and ran.

6

FALL WAS GETTING ON AND FALL IS THE BEST TIME of year in Kentucky. Spring, when the dogwood and magnolia and redbud are out, is the best time too, and so is summer when it's all hot and lazy out and the days are so long you think they are never going to end and you don't want them to. It's generally the best time of year in Kentucky though winter isn't so much because it rains a lot. Some years we get some snow and the ground is all covered but only for a little while.

I've been in lots of other states, Virginia, Tennessee, North Carolina, and even up north in Indiana and Ohio, because Cincinnati, which is just across the Ohio River from Ashland, is really in Ohio. I think they are all right if you are born in them, in one of them I mean. Probably people who live in them get used to them, but I like Kentucky better than all of them put together.

My father goes to all kinds of places and he doesn't seem to mind, but Mr. Kinney at the farm has never been out of Kentucky. He's never even been to Louisville and doesn't want to go there. My uncle went to medical school in Boston and then he was an interne in a hospital there and later what they call a resident in a big medical center in New York. He knows lots of Yankees and he says some of them are all right and can't be blamed for what their ancestors did in the war, but I don't know. He says the only real difference between the North and Kentucky is that it is cold up there and he doesn't like that and they can keep it.

I went out to the farm for a couple more weekends and then nothing happened for a while. My father went to a librarians' meeting in San Francisco and my mother went to New York. I thought they were about as far apart as they could get. Even my Uncle Henry was away. First he went quail hunting down state with one of his friends from the mountains and then he went to give some lectures at the university in Lexington. He does that every year. Between that and his practice I hardly saw him.

Miz Liz and I had the big house to ourselves the way we sometimes do. It was empty and quiet but we like it that way. I didn't stay in my room so much. Nights we looked at television some but mostly we just sat by a fire in the sitting room we like best and talked. Miz Liz told me about old times and I never get tired of that.

One of the best things you can do in fall is walk through the leaves fallen off the cottonwoods, poplars and maples. They crackle when you step on them and rustle against your legs. I like the smell and feel of them as well as the sound. The trees were getting bare down by the river though the leathery brown leaves stayed on the oaks.

I went down there with Cicero most days when it didn't rain and sometimes even when it did. I set my cage trap that catches squirrels and rabbits without hurting them. For several nights I got nothing but the next morning I saw the gray fur in the trap when I was twenty feet away. Cicero rushed up and barked at it hard. That's just like him. He'll bark at anything he sees like that even before he knows whether its a field mouse or an elephant.

It wasn't either one. It was a small opossum. I've caught 'possum before and mostly they were bigger with coarse brown hair and their ratlike tails and pointed faces and ugly fangs. This was a young one and his coat was pretty. I could have shot him. I had my .22 with me as I usually have when I go to the woods, but I didn't want to, especially when he looked at me. Most 'possums won't. They play dead. I don't know whether he saw me or not because they can't see well in the daytime, but I think he did. After he took a good look he closed his eyes and settled himself and seemed to go to sleep.

I opened the trap so he could get out when he wanted and got Cicero quiet, and we went off to look for a hedgehog I know. We couldn't find him but I found the hole at one end of his burrow and closed it with dirt and branches so he would have to come out the other end. Then Cicero and I sat down to wait for him to come up.

Hedgehogs are varmints. You get them into a cornfield and they'll do plenty of damage and the same in a garden. I don't mind shooting a hedgehog so I cocked my rifle and looked to see that there was a cartridge in the breech and waited some more. The hedgehog didn't come out. He may have been watching. You can't tell about animals. They often watch you when you don't even know they are around. That's one of the things I like about them.

It was a pretty day and the sun was warm though not as warm as it had been a few weeks back. Cicero was rooting and sniffing for rabbits and happy to be out and so was I. Once in a while he sounded, pretending he'd found something but I know him so I knew he hadn't.

If he was in there, the hedgehog didn't plan to come out. If he wasn't home, he could see he had visitors he didn't want so he stayed away. I went back to look at the trap.

The little opossum could have come out any time he liked but he was still there. The spot was warm and sunny. Opossums usually sleep in the daytime, and he probably thought this was as good a place to sleep as any. Probably it was better than where he usually slept. He looked at me again and I looked back. Cicero didn't like it. He gets jealous easily, but I held him back. He was glad when we started back to the house.

Every hour or so I went back to see that the little opossum was all right. I took him a pan of water and a piece of bread, but he didn't move. He stayed in that open trap all day. After dark I took a flashlight and went back again. He was gone and so was the piece of bread, and the pan was upside down. So he'd had his breakfast or dinner or whatever he thought it was before he started out for the night.

One day after school I decided not to go right home. I got some chili and then kept on going downtown and went all the way to the medical center where my uncle has his office. It's a big building with a lot of doctors' offices in it and laboratories and x-ray places and things like that, and it smells the way those places usually do. The big parking lot is always crammed with cars and people keep going in and out. Some of them are lame or have bandages or are in wheelchairs, which is why there are ramps as well as steps at the entrances.

I climbed the stairs to my uncle's office. It's really three offices — a reception room, a room where my uncle has his desk, and a room off that, all white with a kind of high cot on wheels that folds in places and lights on stands and glass cases full of shining knives and other instruments. My uncle's diplomas and licenses are all on the walls in there in thin black frames. Some of them are in Latin. My uncle keeps them there because it gives patients something to look at if they are alone for a few minutes. If you are in a place like that without any clothes on and can see the knives, it makes you a little nervous sometimes.

Sometimes the reception room is so full you can't find a place to sit, but it wasn't office hours so it was empty except for my uncle's assistant. She's a nurse so she wears a white dress and one of those nurse's caps, and she's very, very pretty, even prettier than the last nurse who isn't there any more.

She looked up when I came in. "Why, Verge!" she said. She comes from Athens, not the Greek one but the one in Georgia, so she speaks softly and slower than we do in Kentucky. "Your uncle isn't in, you know. He's in Lexington today."

"I know," I said.

"You didn't come just to see me, did you?" Miss Susan — her full name is Miss Susan Vaughan — laughed.

"Yes, I did," I said. This wasn't really true but when people are as pretty as Miss Susan you have to be polite.

"How nice!" Miss Susan had been working on some papers, but she pushed them to one side of her desk and stood up. "Sit down and we'll talk. Would you like some coffee? I was just going to have some. No, I tell you what. I'll make you some cocoa, and I'll have coffee."

She went into the other room, where there is always a glass pot of coffee on an electric burner, and put water in a stainless steel container to boil on another burner and got a tin of cocoa out of a drawer. I watched her and carried the cups back into the outer room.

It was good cocoa and I'd walked a long way. I know what Miss Susan likes to talk about, so we talked about Uncle Henry and all the things he does. Then we talked about the farm because she's been out there lots of times and about Scalpel and Stethoscope.

We talked a long time. Then I said, "Is it all right if I go in and see *him?*"

Miss Susan made a face. "Do you like *him* better than me?"

"No," I said, "but he's different."

She really laughed this time. "I hope so! Of course you may."

I went into my uncle's room and opened a door in the corner.

My uncle has a skeleton in his closet. I know that is what people say when they mean someone has something to hide, but I mean that he really does have a skeleton and it's in the closet in his office.

I don't know how it is in your family but in ours my grandfather was my uncle's father, and my grandfather was a doctor before he became governor and things like that. Probably he always was a doctor because I don't think that is something you get over, and when my grandfather was in medical school he was the favorite student of an old professor of anatomy. When that professor died he left my grandfather this skeleton he used for demonstrations. That is how my uncle got it.

My uncle likes that skeleton. He says that when he doesn't quite know what to tell some patient who doesn't really have much the matter with him he says, "Excuse me a moment" and goes into the closet and looks at the skeleton which hangs there from a wire. That helps him think of something and he goes back and tells the patient and prescribes some medicine and tells him to take it three times a day.

He uses the skeleton for other things too. Sometimes when he has to set a broken bone he goes into the closet and studies it because a whole skeleton is better than any picture in a medical book. Other times he uses it just for himself. He says that if he gets conceited the skeleton reminds him that is all he amounts to, and if he gets discouraged, it tells him that everybody gets to be a skeleton in the end.

I've known the skeleton ever since I was little, and I like it. Once it was someone who walked around and talked and ate his meals and went to bed at night, but I don't know who he was or where or when, just that it was a long time ago. I've learned things from the skeleton too. I know the names of some of his bones and I know I have some just like his.

"That skeleton is all right," my uncle told me once. "Doesn't talk too much, doesn't offer any advice, minds his own business and yet makes a conclusive comment on the whole human race."

"Yes," I said, though I didn't know everything he meant.

7

WHEN MY MOTHER CAME HOME SHE WAS ALL excited. She'd seen a lot of people she wanted to see in New York and bought a lot of new clothes. I thought she'd never stop telephoning. She told everybody about everything but always said she was glad to get home because she'd missed her family so much and they had missed her so. I'd never heard of that before. I didn't listen on purpose because I wouldn't do that, but I heard it every time I tried to call and ask her things over my green telephone but couldn't because she was always talking to somebody.

My father was excited too. In San Francisco he'd bought a first edition of a book called *A Week on the Concord and Merrimack Rivers,* which was printed in 1849, and he was sure it was a copy Ralph Waldo Emerson had taken to California with him in 1871. He was so pleased he even showed the book to me. It was kind of a dirty brown and didn't look like much. He was writing letters to other book people trying to find out more about it.

He brought me a good new compass on a strap like a wristwatch, and I was glad to have it. I didn't need it to find my way there but I wore it to school for a while to get used to it. Then I put it back into its box to take with me the next time I went to the farm and could really practice with it in case I got lost in the woods.

Thanksgiving came and went. We don't pay too much attention to it as Thanksgiving is really a northern kind of holiday about the Pilgrims and the Puritans. They never came to Kentucky and I'm glad the Puritans didn't. Then something happened that I really did pay attention to and quite a lot of attention was paid to me.

Our class was going to have StuCom again, which is what everybody calls it when he doesn't call it something worse, and it was my turn this time. The StuCom is for "Student Community." It's a kind of public speaking with, what the principal says is, "audience participation." You talk about what you do or think or make outside of school, sharing your talents with the school community. Those are the things the principal says and what the teachers say after him because he says it. I wouldn't want anyone to think I talk that way. It's just the old Show-and-Tell stuff with a bigger name. Half the things people do are just bigger names for what they did when they were kids anyway.

I guess I really got my idea from Margaret Hobart. She'd wanted to talk about human beings so I thought I would only differently. I don't like getting up in front of the class and showing off but it's easier if it is something you're really interested in. I told my Uncle Henry about my idea and asked him if I could.

My idea was to take the skeleton to school and tell about his bones.

Uncle Henry thought about it. Then he said, "I don't know why not. He hasn't been out in a long time. A little fresh air will be good for him. I'll bring him home for you."

He brought the skeleton in one of those leather and canvas bags people use for coats and dresses when they are traveling. It was a good long one and the skeleton just fitted. No one else was around at the time so we just hung the bag in the big closet in my room.

My uncle said he would drive me to school the day of the StuCom. I was glad of that because you can't take a skeleton on a school bus when it is full of people shouting, and it was too far to carry it and walk.

I really studied that skeleton every night for a week and I read parts of a book my uncle lent me. I learned a lot. I got it down pretty good and I practiced my speech on Cicero. He

42

listened because he likes me but I don't think he understood very much. I know he likes the skeleton too because he doesn't bark at it.

The morning my uncle drove me to school I hung the skeleton in the traveling bag in the cloak room and told the teacher it was a secret and I didn't want anyone to touch it. Some of the other kids had brought stamp collections and budgerigars in their cages, pet turtles and things like that. One boy had a sword his great-grandfather had in the War Between the States, and a girl had a picture she had painted by coloring the numbers in a pattern. All morning while we had regular classes everybody was kind of excited and I was a little.

StuCom was after lunch. First a girl showed a pair of silly lovebirds in their cage and told how they loved each other but they didn't seem to. Then a boy showed a little table he had made out of pine wood and told how he'd sawed and planed the wood and then sanded it. We all knew his father had made most of it so no one cared.

I got really interested though when Gladys Hardman showed a little totem pole that her father, who is in the Air Force, brought her from Alaska. She told what all the carvings on it meant and about the Indians who made it. I got so interested I forgot it was my turn next and jumped when the teacher called on me.

Probably that was good because it kept me from being nervous. I went to the cloak room and brought back the long bag. Then I stood on a chair and hung the bag on the hook that holds up the big map of the United States. I was sweating a little when I got down off the chair and I stopped for a minute to get my breath.

Then I reached up and unzipped the bag and the cover rolled back and fell to the floor and the whole thing showed.

"This is my uncle's skeleton," I said.

The teacher drew in her breath with a noise. That was the only sound. The class was staring but two girls had their hands over their eyes.

"Oh, I don't mean it's *his* skeleton, but it's his," I said, "and he said I could bring it to show you."

Of course everybody has seen make-believe skeletons on television and plastic ones at Hallowe'en and things like that, but my skeleton was real. You could see right off that it had a man around it once.

"He's killed his uncle!" yelled Tommy Marquis, "and now he's brought him here!" He jumped up and ran out of the room. Two other boys ran after him just to make a fuss while they could.

Helen Maller began to cry and so did Jane Housman.

"Children, we must not panic!" the teacher said. She was very white. "Everybody stay in their seats!" (That's bad grammar, but she was excited.)

"I want to go home! I want to go home!" That was Vicky Anderson.

Johnny Tibbets had his eyes closed, and he was all shrunk back in his seat. Sonny Craig was too. A girl was on the floor. I think she'd fainted.

The skeleton just hung there and looked at them. That's what I did. I forgot all I was going to tell them about him.

"Don't be afraid, children! Don't be afraid!" said the teacher. Then she put her handkerchief over her mouth and ran out the door.

In a minute there were heavy footsteps, and the principal put his head in. He didn't come all the way in. He didn't dare, and it showed. He is partly bald and fat in the middle, and the bottom part of his face is fat. My mother says he is wonderful because he understands boys. Maybe he does, but he doesn't understand skeletons.

"Call his father," I heard him order a teacher who was trying to look over his shoulder the way Billy Allen was trying to see between his legs. "See if he is all right! See if anyone else is missing!"

"It's only my uncle's skeleton," I said, "and he's not missing. He's at the clinic right now."

The principal really took charge then. He backed out into the hall and shouted, "Fire drill! First row form a line! Second row follow. Then — "

Nobody formed any lines. The class rushed out and knocked him down and ran all over him. By this time all the other classes were out in the hall too, everybody running and shouting and having a good time. I was alone in the room with the skeleton when I heard the siren and the tires screaming as the police car skidded up.

The cops roared for people to make way then burst into the room with their guns in their hands. It was Mike Hathway and Harry Winner. They're friends of my uncle's and see him at accidents and the revolver club.

"What's going on here?" said Mike before he saw who it was.

Harry was just standing staring at the skeleton. "It's a beauty," he said. "I never saw one as good as that one."

Mike closed the door. It was quiet then, quieter anyway, and he came over to look.

"It looks like old Jake Simmons who used to live down Four Corners way," he said.

"More like the way Skinny Beaumont looks now," said Harry. Mr. Beaumont has a hardware store on Breckenridge Street.

"I didn't kill anybody," I said.

"Course not," said Mike. "Takes years to make a good skeleton like this. Where'd you get him?"

I told them and they listened. I wasn't going to waste all my speech either. I told them about the skull and the ulna and the tibia and the pelvis and things, and they asked me a couple of questions.

"What are we going to do now?" asked Harry.

"I don't know, but we got to make it look good. You don't mind, do you, Verge? I'll put the cuffs on you. They're busted so they won't bother you none. Then we'll get out of here."

So Harry zipped up the skeleton and carried it, and Mike followed with his gun on me and they pushed our way through the hall, which was still in an uproar. They put the skeleton and me in the police car and started the siren and drove us home.

I hung the skeleton back up in the closet in my room while Miz Liz gave Mike and Harry coffee and cake in the kitchen. When I went back they were telling her all about it.

"Don't know what school's coming to these days," Miz Liz was saying, "and that principal's a foreigner from Alabama or one of those places. He won't ever make a decent skeleton. Too fat."

"Too stupid too," said Mike.

I thought I'd better tell my mother before someone else did, so while they were still talking I went back to my room and listened on my green telephone.

". . . dear old Miss Dorothy for our guest of honor," she was saying, "and Cecilie Jones can show those wonderful pictures she took in Hawaii showing the plight of the natives, and . . ."

"Mother, I got arrested this afternoon," I said.

"That's nice, dear," said my mother, "but can't you see, darling, that mother's busy. Now run off and play."

"That's what I've been trying to do," I said and hung up.

Miz Liz gave me an extra big piece of cake and a glass of milk when I went back into the kitchen and Harry showed me his hand gun. It's a .38 Special and a good one. Mike carries a Colt Woodsman with a six-inch barrel because he says he can't hit anything with a Police Positive. I told him I liked a Smith & Wesson target revolver like my uncle's better, and I think I hurt Mike's feelings a little.

There was a big piece on the front page of the paper that night. It said that the principal was a hero because he had quelled a near panic at the school and no one had been injured because of his calm and courage. My name was in it and it said I was the son of the eminent Professor Oliver Trewbridge and the nephew of the famed surgeon Dr. Henry Trewbridge and that my mother was the Social and Civic Leader Sybil Trewbridge. It said my brother was a graduate of the University of Virginia but nobody had seen him in a long time. An investigation would soon get under way to find out whether the skeleton had died a natural death.

I hid the paper. I didn't even show it to Miz Liz. Sometimes if you don't think about things they go away.

I forgot they'd called my father at the college. As soon as he came home he came straight to my room, which he never does. Cicero jumped up and began to bark at him because he thought he was a stranger.

My father didn't even take off his glasses. He looked at me right through them.

"Have you been murdering anyone lately?"

I told him I hadn't.

He said that was good and asked me where I'd got the cadaver.

I told him it wasn't a cadaver but a skeleton and opened the closet door and showed him.

"Why, I know him!" he said and seemed quite pleased. "I used to wonder whether he was an Indian or someone who was hanged. See where the neck has been broken and mended?"

He got quite interested. I hadn't thought about that so I was interested too. My father and I got quite friendly for a few minutes before he took off his glasses and told me not to blow up the school or burn it down and went away.

I took Cicero then and went down into the fields and we poked around. I knew we were going to eat in the dining room that night and that my uncle was coming. I thought I'd better keep out of sight until then. I was right too.

Somebody had told my mother as I knew someone would. She was all sort of fainty when she came into the dining

room and she'd got another copy of the newspaper somewhere. She didn't look at me but right at my uncle as the girl,
who helps Miz Liz but doesn't sleep in, brought the soup.

"You've seen this, of course," she said, passing the
folded newspaper over to him.

"Oh, yes. Nice bit of publicity. I'll see Ed Bucknell first
thing in the morning and put a stop to it." Mr. Bucknell is the
editor of our newspaper.

"What will you do?" I asked him.

"Ought to take out his larynx, perhaps his epiglottis too.
Keep him from talking too much."

"It suggests that Vergil killed his dear brother Hamilton!"
My mother began to cry.

"Don't know why he hasn't," said my uncle.

"This is delicious pea soup, Miz Liz," my father said.

"Ought to be," said Miz Liz. "Got a good ham bone in it."

"That's all the skeleton is," I said. "Bones."

"Be still, Vergil!" said my mother. "At the dinner table!"

"Now, Sybil," said my father.

It *was* good soup. I'd finished mine and was licking my
spoon.

My mother stopped crying so she could attack my uncle
some more. "I don't think you are a fit associate for our son,"
she said.

"Fit? Miz Liz and Verge and I are the only fit people
around. Oliver isn't fit enough to walk a quarter of a mile.
You are fit for many things, Sybil, but not for some others."

"Am I to sit here and be insulted at my own table?"

"Don't insult her," my father said to my uncle, "though I
really don't think you did."

"I don't either," I said.

"Be still!" my mother shouted at me. "You've brought disgrace on your whole family again! If only your brother were
home!"

That's when my father stopped it all. "He will be," he said.

"A letter came at the college today. As usual he wants more money. He said they might come home for Christmas."

My mother pressed her hand to her chest and gave a cry. "How wonderful! Hamilton home for Christmas! Really, I can't stand any more. I must ask you to excuse me." She stood up.

"Sit down and eat your dinner, Sybil," my father said.

My mother sat down hard. I was surprised. The roast beef and sweet potatoes were just as good as the pea soup, and my mother ate just as much as the rest of us.

8

WHEN I WENT BACK TO SCHOOL MONDAY ALL THE kids looked at me. The fellows were jealous because none of them ever was taken out of school by the cops in handcuffs and at gun point. The girls looked at me as if I were molasses taffy. Even the teacher was all smiles. She told the class they should be proud to have someone in it with such advanced scientific interests.

Mr. Bucknell, you see, had put another piece in the paper. It explained things and said my brother was really alive and was coming home from his advanced studies in Europe just to spend Christmas with his remarkable family. I don't think my uncle even had to take out Mr. Bucknell's tonsils to make him do it either. Probably the editor owes him money. He owes most people.

It's funny how people change, but I didn't pay any attention. If they didn't like me one day, they didn't have to try so hard a couple of days later. I let them see it didn't make no never mind to me. After school I went for my chili and French fries. Tony, who runs the place, probably never looks at the newspapers so he didn't say anything more than he usually does, and I went home feeling all on fire from the chili. It's a good way to feel.

I told my uncle he could take the skeleton back any time but he said no. He said I had to give back the traveling bag he was in because he had borrowed that from Miss Susan but I could keep the skeleton.

"I've got about everything out of him I need. Besides, you've earned him. I wish I'd been there. You're doing all right. I never got arrested until I was a lot older than you are."

"They didn't take me to jail."

"Don't sound so disappointed! Probably they will next time."

I felt pretty proud. No one ever gave me a skeleton before. I have a skeleton in *my* closet now. When we're not busy Cicero and I sometimes get a little lonely. He'd be company.

I showed him to Miz Liz.

"Thought I knew most people around these parts," she said, "but I don't think I knew him. Probably was another no-count. You keep him dusted. I got enough to do without waiting on him. Hungry? I made gingerbread and it's still warm. Of course, it isn't much without whipped cream so I whipped up some. Come on." She didn't have to call me twice.

It didn't seem any time then until Christmas was coming and I began to help Miz Liz the way I do every year. We always have a big crowd of people, kinfolk and friends, over the holidays, and we were going to have more than ever so there was plenty to do.

You can buy mincemeat in the stores but Miz Liz says it isn't fit to eat and she makes her own. So I cut up the dried peel, pounds of it, and she mixed it with the other stuff and put it in big jars. Some people use brandy in it but Miz Liz uses bourbon. I don't like the taste of it, but I like the smell while I'm cutting peel with a sharp old hunting knife and eating plenty as I go along.

There's a fireplace in almost every room in our house. I carted in wood for all of them. I went with my uncle in the Rover and we brought a load of meat and vegetables from the farm, pork roasts and sausage meat and yams and potatoes and apples. There were quail and doves in the freezer.

Miz Liz hired a couple more women to help her the way she does different times, and they redded up the whole house. They stay to help her right along till after New Year's, and we really need them. We have a lot of kinfolk who live off a ways, and they all come, and then there are other people I don't know and never see between Christmases.

I got my shopping done. I got an old book for my father in a secondhand store. It was the oldest one the man had and coming apart in places, but I glued it some. Then in one of the big discount stores I got three gold-looking pens for eighty-nine cents for my mother. She's always writing, and I thought they'd match her French telephone even if it said on the box they were made in Taiwan.

You can't give Miz Liz things like that, and I wouldn't. It has to be something you do yourself. This year I'd been planning a long time, and I had something special. A red fox had been raiding the chickens out at the farm so Mr. Kinney had trapped it and shot it, which served it right. It had a good coat. My uncle skinned it and said it would make a fine woman's scarf. He knows a place where they cure pelts so we took it there, and the man promised it would be ready for Christmas. I kept counting the days, not the way kids do until Christmas but until that fur would be ready for Miz Liz.

The big problem was Margaret Hobart. I don't really want to give her anything, but I always do. Usually I give her a handkerchief or a notebook or something, but you can't keep doing that. I thought about perfume, but Miz Liz said that unless it costs a lot it isn't any good. They have sweet-smelling soap in the drug store, but if I gave her that she'd say I was saying she needed a bath. I know her. Besides, it wouldn't be true. Whatever else Margaret Hobart is, she's always clean.

"Do you think I should get her a bikini?" I asked Miz Liz. "The girls all have them and they ought to be cheap this time of year."

"Look cheap to me any time," said Miz Liz. "Remember I can't give you anything this year. Been too busy."

"That's all right," I said.

Miz Liz says that every year, but nights a couple of times she put her knitting away quick when I came in. I knew what she was making. Miz Liz knows a place way down in the hills where they have the best and warmest wool. They use vegetable dyes, and Miz Liz says it is the only place she can get a true madder red.

She said madder red so many times I knew my sweater and mitts would be red this year. I didn't mind that. Miz Liz makes the softest and warmest sweaters anybody makes, and I already have the black one and the heather one and a blue one without sleeves. They fit too. Sweaters Miz Liz makes make store-bought ones look like trash, which mostly they are.

Well, I couldn't make Margaret Hobart a sweater because I can't knit. I thought if Cicero had pups I would give her one, but I know he won't. It was getting later and later so I was getting really worried, though I think Margaret Hobart is the last thing I should worry about. She wasn't spending her time in Richmond worrying about me.

The house smelled good all the time as Miz Liz baked all day long. It got to be less than a week before Christmas, almost time for me to break the eggs for Miz Liz. We always have a great silver bowl of eggnog on the table in the front hall to give callers when they come. Miz Liz puts bourbon in that too, plenty of it. Then she sprinkles a kind of fine red dust on it. Uncle Henry and I brought the milk and eggs in from the farm so they would be ready.

Then I did what I always save till last. The Saturday before Christmas I took my .22 out to the farm. It was a sunny day after a dark cold spell, and the place I was going is a long way from the farmhouse. I was really going hunting this time so I took a sack with me, a big one. I liked walking across the fields and so did Cicero.

I know a place on the side of a hill near the woods where there are seven big black walnut trees. The squirrels get most of the nuts, but I get plenty too. I'd already done that and shelled them and shelled a bushel of pecans for Miz Liz for pecan pie. This time I was after something else.

Mistletoe grows on black walnut trees. It grows way up high and out at the end of big branches. You can't climb to get it because it is out of reach. What you have to do is shoot it down. Some people use shotguns, but I wouldn't do that. It shatters the mistletoe clusters. I use my .22.

What I do is lie on my back on the ground and steady the rifle on my elbows or a log. That would be cheating at a turkey shoot, but it isn't cheating when you are picking mistletoe for Christmas. I aim at the twigs holding the mistletoe to the tree. They are small but they are black when you are looking into the sky. When you take very careful aim and squeeze your shot off you can cut the twig as clean as with a knife, and the bunch of mistletoe falls to the ground.

I didn't hit the twig every time but mostly I did. Cicero wagged his tail and sort of cheered every time a good piece of mistletoe dropped. He knows about it just as well as I do.

The mistletoe was good this year and there was plenty of it. I used up almost a whole box of bullets but by the time I was through I had my sack full. I like mistletoe. The big white berries are waxy and smooth and the leaves are dark green and glossy. I gave some to Mr. and Mrs. Kinney and then I got a ladder from the barn to cut the holly. It was lucky I had kept the squirrels away from it. There wasn't too much with berries on the tree because the robins get them too and you can't shoot robins, but the ones there were a bright red. I cut some branches that had no berries from the male tree so as not to damage the female too much.

The leaves of a farm holly are not as dark and shiny as those from nursery hollies. They are a kind of sage green. There are other kinds but that is what we have in Kentucky. You have to use a sharp knife or shears and cut about a half-inch from where the twigs branch. No matter what you do, you get scratched by the sharp points of the leaves, but that doesn't matter because holly is beautiful.

It took me a long time, mostly because I felt so good that I made what I was doing last. About the middle of the afternoon my uncle drove me home in his big car. He was wearing a suit and white shirt and his bow tie because he was going to the medical center. He said he'd be back at dinner when he dropped me off at our house. I took the sack of mistletoe and the big armful of holly in to Miz Liz. She thought they were fine.

I looked at the big Christmas tree my mother and her friends had been decorating in the drawing room. It seemed to me she had more women than ever around her and was making even more of a fuss over them than usual. They had the tree all smothered with tinsel and ornaments but I didn't think much of it. It didn't come from Kentucky but from way off somewhere. Besides, I don't think people should cut down millions of firs that probably took twelve years or more to grow. If people want Christmas trees, I think they should grow them in pots and keep them, not just kill them. My mother and all the other women were talking so much and so loudly they didn't see me.

I was going to wash up then but Cicero and I were so tired we didn't make it. We went to our room and fell asleep. When I woke it was dark and what woke me were different voices in the front hall. For a minute I was confused the way you are when you wake, but then I knew whose the loudest voice was and I made a face in the dark. There's always something to spoil everything. I went out to look.

My mother came rushing down from her room when she heard my brother's voice and threw her arms around him. "Hamilton! Hamilton! It's been almost two years! How I have longed for this moment!"

My brother kissed her, but then he wriggled away and arranged his hair at the hall mirror with both hands because she had mussed it.

My mother held out her hand to the girl, who had come with him, the way she does to guests she doesn't know very well. The girl didn't take it. She said, "Hi," and sat down on the floor and looked around.

Mother told my brother his room was just as he had left it, but she said he would be sharing my bathroom. "We are going to be so crowded for the holidays," she apologized to him. She didn't apologize to me.

I said all right because I knew I'd have to anyway.

"Lucille just cleaned that bathroom," said Miz Liz. She had come into the hall and was watching.

"Hello, Liz, old girl," said my brother. "You still around?"

I wanted to kick him. He and Miz Liz always hated each other.

I know you are supposed to love your brother. I don't love mine. I don't like him; I never liked him, and probably I never will like him, and that's all I'm going to say about it.

At dinner my brother and the girl ate as if they were starved, but that didn't stop my brother from talking. He gave a kind of lecture about Paris and Geneva and Rome and those places and told how wonderful they were and how wonderful he was and all the wonderful things he and the girl had done. He made it sound as if he had done everything by himself, but I knew he hadn't because my father kept sending Hamilton money, lots of it.

The girl didn't say much. She just kept her eyes on Hamilton as if he were pecan meats dipped in powdered sugar and even more wonderful than she thought and chewed and swallowed and asked for more and chewed and swallowed some more. My mother watched Hamilton the same way the girl did.

My uncle kept looking at my brother too but not the way the girl and my mother did. Once he spoke to him. "Pass the salt, please," he said. When dinner was over, Uncle Henry asked to be excused, winked at me, and left.

56

9

PEOPLE BEGAN TO COME FROM ALL OVER NOW. There is a wide curved drive that comes to our front door so people can get out of their cars at the pillars and then another curve around the house where people can park their cars on the grass. It began to fill up. Most of the cars were from Kentucky, but there were two each from Tennessee and Virginia and one from Indiana and one from Illinois.

Of course, they didn't come by themselves. There were two or three people in every one of them, Trewbridges, McGowans, Keillers, Hobarts and others. My mother was all dressed up and greeting people, and my father was dressed up sort of too. Miz Liz wore dark, silk-looking dresses all the time, and the other two women had frilly white aprons and hats. The noise was something, and if everybody wasn't happy to see everybody else and didn't say so at the top of her voice, I don't know which one it was. I knew some of them and some I kind of remembered I had seen before, but others I had never even heard of. There was one kid too, and I was told to be nice to him.

More people came to call because the other people came and they wanted to see them, and because it was a party. They were people from town and around. Honestly, you'd have thought it was Derby Day except that it was winter and there were no horses. The day before Christmas — they call it Christmas Eve but it was only about four o'clock in the afternoon when it began — there was a big cocktail party with a lot of women who dressed like my mother and sort of looked like her. The big drawing room was jammed, and they were all laughing and drinking and talking at once. I stayed in the kitchen and sampled things off all the trays of little make-believe sandwiches and tiny cakes the women helping Miz Liz kept taking in. When they pushed through the doors with their trays the noise got louder, then cut off as the doors swung closed.

Margaret Hobart's mother came all dressed up and the aunt from Richmond and even Margaret Hobart's father. He has a deep voice and laughs a lot and knows everybody because he is a salesman. They had two young women with them, but I could hardly see them through the crowd and I'd seen all I wanted anyway. I ate a couple more of the make-believe sandwiches with something fishy on them and poured myself another glass of cider.

Then one of the young women I'd glimpsed pushed through into the kitchen. She had a cocktail glass in her hand and her hair all fixed and it was Margaret Hobart.

"Hi, Verge," she said. "Isn't this just too quaint? What did you get me for Christmas?"

"Hello," I said.

"I don't wonder you didn't know me. I was just a child when I left here. I'm thirteen now. That makes me three years older than you."

It doesn't, and Margaret Hobart knows it because I'll be eleven in February, but if that's the kind of arithmetic they have in Virginia, it's all right with me.

"What makes you think I'm going to give you anything tomorrow?" I said.

"I brought you something all the way from Richmond," she said and took a sip out of her glass. "It's not a real cocktail," she said. "It's just Coke. Isn't that silly? We have cocktails all the time at school and at my aunt's."

"I thought they looked kind of drunk," I said. I didn't want to say I thought *she* sounded drunk because I didn't want her getting mad all over the place.

She knew what I meant though, so she said, "I must be getting back to the other grownups," and she went back in.

She left the door open, and I could see my brother in the middle of the floor stroking his beard and talking loudly to a circle of people around him. He'd found some different clothes somewhere, and I guess my mother had bought the girl some because she had on a blue jean skirt.

"Christmas is really only a pagan festival," I heard my brother say, "but a charming peasant tradition."

Seeing Margaret Hobart made me know I'd better hurry so I went back to my room. Cicero was out so the skeleton and I had the place to ourselves, and we were far enough away so that the roar was just a murmur when I shut the door.

I still felt sorry for Margaret Hobart because it was partly my fault she has to stay in Virginia so I'd bought her a book about Kentucky in the same shop where I'd got the book for my father. I wasn't sure the book was just right to keep her from forgetting where she belongs so I'd written a poem called "Kentucky" to go with it. It was only four lines and I had it all written out, but it didn't look very good so I had to copy it once more. I'd found a piece of good white paper in the library when my father was out. When I pressed it down hard I could see through it to the lines on a piece of school paper I had underneath so I could get the lettering straight.

It took a long time but I got it perfect. Then I signed it and put the date of Christmas Day on it and folded it into a long envelope and put it into the book. Then I got the long box with the fox fur out of the closet with the skeleton, where I'd put it because Miz Liz doesn't go in there, and opened it and looked at it for the hundredth time. I'd had it for three days and had an awful time not telling her.

It was beautiful. The man said I didn't have to pay him because Uncle Henry had taken care of that, which was a good thing as probably I didn't have enough money, and I'd walked all the way home with it. I was glad it was in a box with tissue paper in it and a ribbon on it. I like to give people presents, but I hate having to wrap them. Half the time I don't because I can't.

The party was still going on and it was noisier and noisier. It was dark now. I decided to go out and look for Cicero, though he really doesn't need anyone to find him. He always knows his way. The drive as well as the place behind the house was filled with cars now, and there was a man my father had hired to guard them. I know him so I said hello, and he said hello, then I walked down the road away from the house.

It was silent out there the way Christmas is supposed to be. About all I could see when I looked away from the house were the sky and the outlines of bare trees. I walked quite a piece then turned and started back. The lights of our house showed through branches. They got brighter and brighter, but there were no stars and I could smell the rain in the air. We don't have many white Christmases in Kentucky, but there was no snow in Jerusalem or Bethlehem the first Christmas Day, at least I never heard there was. Now our house was blazing with lights and you could hear the noise and the music. Someone was playing the big square piano and people were singing "God rest ye merry, Gentlemen." It sounded good way off there in the darkness.

Cicero had smelled me and came running from somewhere. He pushed his cold nose into my hand. "Merry Christmas, Cicero," I said, and he whined and wagged himself against my shins.

When we got back I took out my uncle's present and tried to wrap it. I had got him a new gun stock the right size for his twelve gauge. It was walnut but with the wood raw so I had sanded it and finished it with coats and coats of boiled linseed oil and turpentine the way Mr. Kinney showed me. It took a long time to dry. Then I checkered the butt. That's the way you do so it won't slip against your shoulder. I didn't do a good job of that. I got the lines crooked and had to do them over. It really wasn't much good but I put on plenty more oil and after it was dry I waxed the whole stock to a good dull glow. I hoped my uncle wouldn't notice the bad checkering; that is, I knew he would but I hoped he wouldn't mind.

Don't try to wrap a gun stock. It's a good shape for a gun but not for wrapping. I tried and tried, but when I got through it looked like a big sausage somebody had been walking on. I took the paper off then and just tied a red ribbon around the grip with a card that said "to Uncle Henry from Verge."

I don't know when the crowd went. Of course, the ones that were staying with us didn't go at all. We didn't have any regular dinner, but I had eaten so much in the kitchen I didn't mind. In fact, I didn't notice it. I wanted to get in and put my presents under the tree with all the other boxes and packages for the morning, but that isn't something you can do with people watching. I tried to stay awake, but I couldn't. That's how I happened to wake early Christmas morning, which is what I wanted to do and always do anyway.

It was still dark so I used my flashlight to find my way and put my things under the tree. I wanted to see what there was for me but I didn't want to turn the lights on. I went back to bed to listen. I didn't mean to but I fell asleep again because the bed was warm and Cicero wasn't up yet. That's where I was when Miz Liz woke me.

"You be quiet and you and I can get some good breakfast in us before these hyenas upstairs come traipsin' down."

When Miz Liz says good breakfast that's what she means. She had it all ready. We had sausage from the farm and hot cakes and grits and cocoa for me. I love grits. Once Miz Liz saw a Yankee put sugar and cream on his grits instead of ham gravy or butter. She's told me lots of times. I think it frightened her.

"You keep growing and a body won't be able to find enough wool in all Kentuck' to make you things," she said, "but this ought to do. It's madder red — true madder."

I put it right on, and it fit perfectly the way things Miz Liz makes always do. Then I ran to my room and got the fox fur.

You should have seen her eyes open. She couldn't say

anything. Then she cleared her throat and wiped her glasses. "Hope it does me more good than it did him," she said. She meant the fox. "It's pretty. It's right pretty!"

"Put it on! Put it on!"

"In the kitchen! I guess I got more sense than that. I don't put him on in any kitchen. When I put him on . . ." She stroked the fur and didn't say anything more. She just filled my cup with more cocoa and gave me a gritty corn stick to finish off with so I knew she really liked the fox. "Now you go clean up," she said. "We got to show these Yankees a thing or two."

They weren't all Yankees upstairs, but Miz Liz calls all strangers Yankees.

I went to brush my teeth and wash and comb my hair, but when I got there I found my brother in my bathroom. We hadn't heard him sneak downstairs.

"Merry Christmas," I said.

He just closed the door on me, but I'd no sooner got back to my room than he was after me.

"Where's your toothpaste?" he said. "I don't have any."

"Don't they use it in Europe?"

"Don't give me any of your sass," he said, just as if he'd never left Kentucky.

I didn't want him using any of mine so I said, "There's a new tube on the shelf in the closet."

He went over and opened the door. Then he screamed. He jumped back, banged his head on the door jamb, and fell on the floor.

I'd forgotten the skeleton was in there. I ran for Miz Liz, and she came. We looked down on my brother.

"Pour some cold water on him," said Miz Liz. "Do him good."

I got a jugful in a hurry and was going to douse him, but by the time I got back to my room the girl was there.

"What have you done to Hamilton, you little barbarian?" she yelled at me. "You know he's sensitive!"

"I didn't do anything," I said. "He did." I pointed to the skeleton, which she hadn't seen.

So there was another scream, but the girl didn't faint. She just ran. My mother must have heard the scream because pretty soon she was in my room. Her hair was all mussed and she had a bathrobe on over her nightdress.

"Must you ruin every day, even Christmas Day?" she asked me. Hamilton was unfainted now, but he looked sick. My mother helped him toward the back stairs.

I'd got my bathroom back and I didn't think my brother would go there again so I took a long hot shower. Then I put on good flannel trousers and polished shoes and a clean white shirt so I wouldn't disgrace the madder sweater. I put it back on and kept it on all day. It made me feel like myself only better.

There was a crowd at breakfast, not as many as the day before, just family, the way they say. My father was kind of quiet but my mother was brilliant. Her eyes were shining and she laughed at everything. There was one old man I liked and a woman who looked warm and kind, but my brother was there with his girl. He was showing all his teeth when he smiled. I was glad there wasn't any of my toothpaste on them.

I didn't want any more breakfast so I didn't eat with them, but then my mother called me to go into the big room with them all to open the presents. She kissed me and hugged me and said Merry Christmas just as if she hadn't seen me before that morning. There was the other boy about my age, but his parents kept him close to them as if they didn't want him to associate with me. He looked at me and grinned.

Everybody began to open paper and toss ribbons around and exclaim over what they had been given and kiss people and say thank you. The other boy's mother and father had brought all his presents to open, and he got a chemistry set and skis and ice skates and other stuff I wouldn't want. I got a lot of clothes and books, but the big thing was a new ten-speed bike. It was made in France with very narrow tires and the whole thing weighed only twenty-five pounds. It was a beauty — red. I knew I could make it go like anything. I said thank you to my mother and father and they said I was welcome and Merry Christmas all over again, and my mother kissed me again.

When Margaret Hobart and her mother and the other girl came they said the rain had started and shook it out of their hair and cried Merry Christmas, and it all began again. My brother's girl was talking to the Richmond aunt and telling her about the skeleton in my closet and Margaret Hobart heard and came running over to me.

She was wearing her first evening gown with a long skirt and she was playing with a yoyo her Richmond cousin had given her. She'd put the gown on as soon as she opened the box under the tree at her house, and she wouldn't take it off all day but she wouldn't stop playing with the yoyo either.

"Verge, show it to me! Show it to me right away!"

"You're supposed to wait till you get your present and then say thank you," I said.

"I don't mean that, silly! I mean the skeleton. I want to see it *now!* Hurry before they stop us!"

So I took her to my room and opened the closet door and showed her the skeleton.

She loved it. "It's quaint!" she said. "It's right quaint!"

"Maybe he was an Indian, Uncle Henry says."

"Couldn't be or the bones would be red," said Margaret Hobart. "Here." She shoved a little parcel in white tissue paper at me. She'd been holding it in her hand but I hadn't seen it.

Sometimes Margaret Hobart speaks so fast or acts so fast you do what she says without thinking. It was a knife and a good one. It didn't have all those things on it that you never use but two strong sharp blades, and one had a sawtooth edge on it for scraping the scales off when you go for bass. That's another thing. Sometimes Margaret Hobart knows more than you think.

64

"This is yours," I said.

I gave her the book with the poem in it. She opened the paper and looked at the book. Then she read the poem. She didn't say anything. She didn't even look at me.

"I guess it isn't any good," I said.

"Thank you, Verge. Merry Christmas," she said then. She didn't say whether she liked her present or not, just, "Do you like my dress?"

"Yes."

"Do you think I'm pretty?"

"Yes, but that's just on top. Underneath you look just like *him*."

"I do not. You do. I'm going to be a beauty soon."

"Who says so?"

"My mother and my aunt, just everyone — and I do too."

"That's good," I said.

Margaret Hobart looked at me hard. She doesn't bat her eyes any more. She just looks. She gave the yoyo a big throw to show how good she is with it. Then she said, "Come on. Let's go back into the other room."

I had my bike and my sweater and my knife, but there wasn't anything from Uncle Henry. I couldn't help wondering. His gun stock was still under the tree too.

Just then my uncle's big car turned in as it began to rain harder. He stopped it right in front of the pillars, and he and Miss Susan jumped out and hurried in. Miss Susan was beautiful. She had on a dress the color of my Christmas sweater, and with her gold hair it looked good. There were raindrops on her hair and on her cheeks as they came in, and everyone looked at her and the men looked glad.

My uncle introduced Miss Susan to some of the others and soon after that Miz Liz told my mother dinner was ready to serve. She'd made me put on a jacket and tie. It was pretty hot but I kept my madder sweater on underneath the jacket.

An old man with white hair said grace. I liked the sound of his voice. He lives in Louisville, on Cherokee Road near the big park. I've been there. I sat next to Miz Liz, and she'd put the other boy the other side of me, and Miz Liz's helpers began to bring in the food.

I kept watching for the things I'd helped Miz Liz make, and there were plenty of them, but I could not see them all because there was so much laughing and talking and exclaiming over the wine and roast fowl and the other things. Margaret Hobart was away down at the other end of the table with her mother and father and her aunt and cousin, and she didn't look at me. I couldn't hear what they were saying. When a lot of people are talking at once I never know what any one of them says.

My plate was piled as high as all the others, and I ate everything on it and more. Everybody did. My mother was talking and laughing and smiling at everybody. The boy next to me didn't say anything for a while, but then he did, and I liked hearing him talk. He came from Franklin, Indiana, and he talked funny the way all Yankees do. He said he was going into junior high school the next year, but he called it junior "h-eye" school. All Yankees say "eye" instead of "ah" the way it should be. Women and girls from the North have high, tight voices that hurt your ears. I tried not to hear them.

Christmas dinner took a long time but, except for the noise, I didn't care. It was raining too hard again for me to try out my new bike. I liked it just as well shining by the tree anyway. Miss Susan, who was sitting next to my uncle, smiled over at me, but Uncle Henry was talking to a man I didn't know on the other side of him. Two men were talking to my father and he seemed to be listening but he wasn't hearing what they said. I can tell. He was thinking hard about something else. I wondered what. I didn't see my brother and the girl because I never looked at them.

I saw the other boy's mother look at us. She was worried because she didn't know what I was talking to him about. I was only telling him about the skeleton and, because he was all right, after dinner I took him to my room to show it to him. He sneaked out because he was afraid his mother would stop him.

He looked at the skeleton a long time without moving. Then he said something else I liked. He said, "I ain't had so much fun sence the hawgs et my little sister!"

He didn't make it up. He says lots of people in Indiana say that, so maybe it isn't as bad up North as I thought. I asked him to say it again and he started too, but his mother called him and he looked scared and went.

I sat down on a chair next to my bed. I wasn't thinking of anything when Miss Susan and my uncle came.

"Thought you'd be here," he said. "Miss Susan has something for you."

She did too. I took off the ribbons and tissue paper and it was a big book about Kentucky Thoroughbreds. It had colored pictures of Man O'War, War Admiral, Whirlaway, Gallant Fox, Citation and the others and their records. It told how Thoroughbreds are raised and trained. It even told what bits and bridles and saddles to use different times.

"Now we have to run out to the farm," my uncle said.

"Why?" I'd thought he was going to stay all day, and I didn't want him to go.

"Have to put a new stock on my shotgun," he said. "I got one for Christmas. It was under the tree, and it's a beauty."

"You did?" I said. "That's good."

"Oh, this is yours," Uncle Henry said. He took a long thick envelope out of the inside pocket of his coat and handed it to me. It had my name on the outside. I supposed it was money and I didn't want my uncle to give me money.

"Thank you," I said. "May I come to the farm with you?"

"No. We have to stop at both the hospital and the office. Cancer and heart ailments and a few other things don't know it's Christmas. They keep on as if it were just another day."

"Open it, Verge! Open it!" Miss Susan said.

I slit the envelope with my new knife, and it wasn't money. It was long folded sheets of paper, mostly printing but with writing in spaces.

"Stethoscope's papers," my uncle said. "He's yours."

I couldn't speak. I knew I should say something but I couldn't think what. I didn't have to. Miss Susan grabbed me and hugged me. Because my face was pressed against her I couldn't see my uncle. I could just hear him say sort of muffled, "You have to gentle and train him."

I broke away from Miss Susan. "We'll win the Derby!" I said. "We'll win the Derby!"

"No, we won't, but you'll have a good horse if you make him a good horse."

"I will! I will! I will!"

10

EVERY YEAR THERE ARE A LOT OF PARTIES AT A lot of houses around Christmas. The people staying at our house went to some of them. Others came to our house. Cars were going in and out all the time. Miz Liz and I had to keep filling up the big bowl of eggnog in the hall and pouring in more bourbon.

The rain had stopped. The sun came out and it was quite warm so I got to try my new ten-speed, and it went just as well as it looked. I tried my old knife and then my new knife on a piece of pin oak, and Margaret Hobart's was the best. I kept looking at the papers that said Stethoscope was mine. I could hardly believe it, and I wondered if anyone had told him yet, but I didn't get a chance to go out and see him right off.

My mother was having a wonderful time. Daughters of the Confederacy and other women like that kept coming to see her, and every day they had kind of meetings in one of the sitting rooms. They talked a lot and seemed all excited. I didn't pay much attention because everyone is excited around Christmas. Not my father though. He just went to the college the way he usually does and sort of kept out of sight the rest of the time, the way I do sometimes.

My brother and the girl didn't. They were both back in their blue jeans again. Mostly when Hamilton wasn't upstairs talking with my mother they just sat and thought and looked at each other or at nothing. I kept away from them. Sometimes my brother and the girl were gone all day and all night. I guess they sat somewhere else.

The boy and his mother and father went back to Indiana the day after Christmas. Two of the cars went back to Louisville. Margaret Hobart and her mother and her aunt and her cousin went back to Richmond. Margaret Hobart said they had to get ready for a big reception there on New Year's Eve. I wished all the others would leave too so things could get back the way they ought to be. You know the saying, Christmas comes but once a year. Probably that's enough.

In my room one night I thought about something I heard my uncle say to my father one evening. They were in the library with the door open just a little while my mother was having another big meeting with other women off in that sitting room. I really wasn't trying to listen and I went away as soon as I knew it was something I wasn't supposed to hear, but I heard it.

My uncle said, "Sybil is reversing the usual procedure. She's retreating from private into public life."

I don't know what my father said or whether he answered at all because Cicero and I had gone by then.

I kept thinking about it in the dark upstairs in my bunk with Cicero breathing under me. Maybe I knew a little what my uncle meant about my mother. I know kids who are showoffs because nobody pays them much mind at home, and they want people to notice them and think they're good.

"Stop it, Cicero!" I said.

He was wriggling and whimpering loud in his sleep. He was dreaming about chasing rabbits or being chased by a bear. Of course, I didn't really know that, but I don't think dogs dream much about school or hitting a rut that is frozen hard on a new bike and flying over the handlebars. So maybe I was wrong about my mother too. She isn't a kid.

Finally all the guests left. Then — I was surprised — so did my mother. I didn't know she was going anywhere, but she had long talks with my father in his library and in her room. Then she packed about fifty dresses and twenty pairs of shoes in six bags. She didn't do it. The two extra girls did it with her telling them how. In one of my father's books I read that when Queen Elizabeth (the real one, I mean) traveled, she took cartloads of costumes. That's how my mother is too.

I heard her telling my brother and the girl how terribly sorry she was to leave when they were there but that the convention in Baltimore was just so important and that she might have something fabulous to tell them when she got back and to ask my father for anything they needed. She said she'd be gone only a couple of weeks.

She kissed me goodbye one morning, and my father drove her to the airport. It seemed funny to pick up my green telephone and not hear anything. I went back to eating in the kitchen with Miz Liz and Cicero, and I liked it better than having all the people around.

My mother had been gone only two days when I heard voices one evening. They were pretty loud, and they came from the library, and the door was wide open this time. It was my father and my brother.

My father said, "No!" and I could tell he meant it.

"But we *need* it," my brother said.

"I have thought this over at some length," said my father. "There has to be a stop to it some time. I have decided this is the time."

"Is money that important to you?"

"You seem to find it important."

"Naturally in a materialistic society . . . ," began my brother.

"Then try getting a job."

"A job!"

"It's been done," said my father. I never heard him talk so sharply before.

"With your reactionary ideas I could hardly expect you to understand, but this is a new world free of antiquated ideas and systems. It belongs to us, not to you!"

"I didn't know anybody owned it," said my father.

"I *must* get back to Europe. Things are going on there, things important for the future!"

"I'm sorry you will be so far away again."

"You're not sorry at all!" said my brother.

My father didn't answer.

"All we need are a few thousand dollars!"

"I think you mean a few thousand more, though that's not what worries me particularly."

My brother sounded relieved. "I'm glad you see it my way after all. We won't need it until the end of the week."

"You misunderstand. No more money."

There was a funny sound. I didn't know what it was at first. Then I did. My brother was choking, almost as if he here trying not to cry. "And you wonder why we hate you!" he shouted after a while.

"I don't wonder about much of anything any more," said my father, but his voice was shaking.

"You wait till Mother finds out about this! You just wait!"

"I'll wait," my father promised. He sounded as if he had put his glasses back on.

Then I heard the library door slam, and my brother and the girl began to whisper in the hall. She was swearing words I wouldn't say. I went into my room and closed the door. When I woke in the morning Miz Liz told me that they were gone, blue jeans, guitar and all. "That girl never washed out a thing all the time they were here," she told me.

My uncle stopped for me that afternoon and I went out to see Stethoscope. I think he had been told for he seemed especially glad to see me. He was in his box stall, and I think he was bored. I told him about everything and then I put a halter on him and took him for a walk in the paddock. I didn't dare take him outside the fence. If he took it into his head to run just because he was glad to be out, I couldn't hold him. The ground wasn't really frozen, but it was brown and hard and I didn't want him falling and cutting a knee or anything.

We stayed out a long time. Then I took Stethoscope back in and brushed him down. He didn't really need it because

Mr. Kinney had done it that morning, but I wanted to. I fooled around in the tack room a long time. It's not a real tack room, just pegs with saddles and bridles on them and an old bureau with currycombs and brushes and petroleum jelly and horse liniment in a corner of the stable by the three box stalls — Scalpel's, Stethoscope's and one empty — but when you are a Thoroughbred owner you have to call things by their right names.

My uncle had bought a new saddle so Scalpel's old one just hung there on a peg. I saddlesoaped it well to get it soft and clean. Then I soaped the new bridle I had for Stethoscope. You have to when leather is new or it gets dried and brittle. I showed it to Stethoscope when I had finished and he sniffed at the bright bit, but he really didn't know what it was and didn't care and just wandered around his stall a little and looked out the high window. He could see Cicero outside, and he wanted to go out and play with him.

I ate at the farm that night. Some of my mistletoe was still up in the dining room, and it still looked fresh. It was only a little over a week but it seemed a long time since I had shot it down. We had a good fire in the farm living room. I watched it a long time, and it made me sleepy, so my uncle called my father and told him I was staying the night. Can you go to sleep before you go to bed, while you are still walking around? I guess you can because I don't remember anything about it. Perhaps I caught it from Stethoscope because he can do that.

I went home in the morning with my uncle who was on his way to his office, and I sort of messed around all day. Every once in a while I wondered where my brother and the girl had gone, and a time or two I thought of my mother and wondered what she was doing in Baltimore. I wondered if my brother and the girl had called her or if my father was still waiting.

Along in the afternoon I took my gun, and Cicero and I went down across the fields to the woods and the river. I didn't shoot at anything. I didn't even want to. I had a sheepskin coat on over my sweater but I could still feel the cold down in the bare trees, and the river had ice along the banks. It was all bare and kind of unfriendly out. I didn't mind that too much but I got hungry.

Miz Liz and I ate thick slices of country ham with cloves in it that night and then mince pie and rat cheese. I was glad the visitors hadn't eaten everything. I even liked some of them now they were gone. We ate a little early because Miz Liz was going out to a thing at the church and was going to wear her fox scarf for the first time. Did it look good when she put it on with her hat and coat!

Cicero and I were watching television in my room when I heard my father come in and go to his library. I wondered where he'd had his dinner or if he'd had any. We watched television for nearly an hour, but the things on it weren't that much so I turned it off. Then all of a sudden the house seemed awfully empty. There wasn't a sound.

Mostly I never do it, but I wondered if my father was reading or just waiting the way my brother said, and I hoped the telephone wouldn't ring long distance from Baltimore. Maybe I also wanted to make sure there was someone in the house besides me and Cicero and the skeleton. I went to the library.

My father looked surprised when I went in. "Did I forget something?" he asked me. "Is there something you want?"

He looked tired and pale. "I don't want anything," I said.

"Oh," he said and looked puzzled, and neither of us said anything for a long minute.

"Miz Liz is out," I said. "Mrs. Wright took her to a thing at the church."

"That's nice," he said. He hadn't taken off his glasses this time so I could see him trying to think of something more to say. He sort of sighed and then he said, "Christmas is a pleasant time of the year, and I think we all enjoyed it. I hope your mother is having a fine time in Baltimore. Oh!"

He grabbed his chest and doubled over. He tried to catch

himself as he passed his desk on the way down but all he did was upset the lamp. He crashed to the floor and lay there as if he were dead.

He wasn't. I knew what to do because I've watched my uncle and he's told me things. I felt my fathers' pulse, and it was there only there wasn't much of it and it was too fast. I grabbed the black telephone and dialed fast. All I got was my uncle's answering service. As quick as I could I dialed the farm, but there was no answer. That meant that Mr. and Mrs. Kinney had gone to bed and my uncle wasn't there.

My father's cheek was cold but his neck was warm. I pushed a big book under his head and yanked his old trench coat off the hook on the back of the door and covered him. Then I rushed downstairs to my own green telephone and looked up a number fast. This time I got Miss Susan where she lives. As quickly as I could I told her.

Usually Miss Susan talks slow and sweet. Not this time. "Stay with him. I'll have the police ambulance right there. It's the fastest. I'm on my way."

In the cabinet in the dining room I got a bottle of brandy and raced back to the library. I didn't look for a glass but jerked out the cork and poured some between my father's lips. I got most of it on his chin but some into his mouth. He was breathing hard. I got another teaspoonful in.

I don't know how she got there that fast but it wasn't too soon for me because I didn't know what to do next. Miss Susan ran upstairs for more blankets. She got down on the floor and listened to my father's heart as she counted his pulse. I heard the ambulance and ran to open the front door.

"In there!" I told the cops. They had a stretcher.

"Emergency ward! Get him there fast!" Miss Susan ordered.

They lifted my father as if he were a log but gently and eased him through the library door, out the front and into the ambulance and got in after him. They roared off with the siren screaming.

"It's bad," said Miss Susan. "They'll look after him at the

hospital but we've got to get Hank. He's back in the hills delivering a baby. There's no phone. You know the roads, and it's raining. Get a heavy coat because it's cold too."

She told me where and I did know. There's no doctor up there and the people are my uncle's friends. They don't know that he's a famous surgeon, only that he's a doctor.

"Is he going to die?" I asked Miss Susan as we jumped into her car.

"Not if we make it there and back in time. Which way?"

We tore into the blackness. It was raining hard and seemed to be raining harder because we were driving into it. "Turn here," I said. Miss Susan turned quickly, and I felt the car skid a little. We were on a straightaway then, and she stepped on it. "Big downhill curve," I said. "Slow a little."

The headlights of her car were bright but their light bounced off the slanting rain, making it silver, and throwing reflections back into our faces. Our high beams were the only lights in the whole night countryside. There were no houses this way. A few minutes later we left the hard road. I knew it was only about three miles now but the mud was slick and shined in our headlights.

"Whatever you do don't stop or go too slow," I told Miss Susan. "We couldn't get started again."

"I won't," she said, and she didn't.

She really knows how to drive. As soon as we got by one place I knew we'd made it because the hill is steep and rocky and rain runs off it. Then I saw the light in the farmhouse, just one dim light for there is no electricity there.

"That's it. We're almost there."

Miss Susan was out of the car and dashing through the rain for the door almost before she stopped her car. The dim light spilled out then cut off as the door closed behind her. She could hardly have been in there a minute before Uncle Henry leaped out, buttoning his raincoat as he ran. He called to me to follow him to his Rover, and I rushed after him.

76

"Things are all right there," he said. "Susan can do what else is necessary and drive herself back."

I've always said my uncle's farm car can do everything but fly and swim. That night it almost did both. My uncle did not say another thing and it's good he didn't because all I could do was hang on as we jolted and swayed down the hill before we hit the hard road. Then we flew. Uncle dodged and cut through traffic as we hit town and swerved around corners to the hospital. He drove right to the brightly lighted front doors, left the Rover where he stopped, ran to the desk, then beckoned to me to follow.

The sign said "Intensive Care." Uncle Henry motioned me to a bench and pushed through some swinging doors.

I was wet and sore and tired and hungry but I didn't know it. All I knew was that my father was in there. I could see his face as I bent over him on the floor and hear his breathing. I kept looking at the doors that my uncle had gone through but they were just brown doors.

"What are you doing here, little boy?" a nurse asked me. "Children aren't allowed in the hospital this time of night or in this section at any time."

"Go away!" I said as hard as I could. "Go away!"

"Well, I never!"

"Go away!" I told her again.

She looked frightened and went. I was afraid she'd be back with a guard.

I needn't have worried. My uncle came first. He was as wet as I was. His face was quiet but white. "He's all right," he said, "or will be. Lucky you were there. You did all right."

"I did? You're sure?"

"I'm never sure of anything, but I'm reasonably sure."

"It was a heart attack, wasn't it?"

"You knew it, didn't you?"

"Sort of."

The nurse who had tried to put me out came back now and she did have a guard with her, but when she saw my Uncle Henry she stopped short.

"Yes, nurse?"

"Oh, nothing! Nothing, doctor."

"Could we get some chili?" I asked my uncle. "I know a place."

"Tony's? Good idea. I could use some."

Nobody except my uncle and the other doctors was allowed to see my father for days, and I kept wondering about him. I hoped he wouldn't die because I was used to having him around. Miz Liz and I were alone again. I asked her if my mother was coming.

She shook her head. "Ain't been told. Your father wouldn't let anyone tell her. Leastways that's what your Uncle Henry says."

"Why not?"

"Knew something like this was bound to happen," she said. "Saw it coming. Known that man since he was a boy."

"Was he like me?"

Miz Liz looked at me. "Some," she said. "You're more like your grandfather, and I knew *him* when *he* was a boy."

"You knew almost everybody when they were boys, didn't you?"

"Not your mother, I didn't," said Miz Liz, and she laughed but not as if she meant it.

11

AS SOON AS THEY WOULD LET ME, I WENT TO see my father. He was in a room by himself now. His face was always thin, but it was thinner and sick looking, and he looked very long under the bedclothes. His eyes were closed so I thought he was asleep. I didn't speak but tiptoed close to the bed to look at him.

Then he opened his eyes but he didn't move his head.

"Do you know where my glasses are?" he said.

"They got broken when you fell," I said. "That is, they came off and one of the cops stepped on them."

He closed his eyes again and seemed to think about that for a while.

"You got sick," I said.

"Just tired," he said. Then he thought of something else and opened his eyes and really looked at me. "Living makes you tired."

I didn't know what to say so I said, "I guess so."

My father closed his eyes once more. Then he said, "Yes."

He didn't want to talk any more so I just sat there and watched him and felt sorry for him. Pretty soon I saw he really was asleep, but I still didn't go. I didn't go until a nurse came and took me away with her.

It was cold out, damp cold that went through your clothes. I went to Tony's for my chili. When I went to pay him, Tony wouldn't take the money. " 's on the house this time," he said. "Your paw's sick, ain't he? Saw it in the paper. He's a good guy."

"I know he is," I said and felt surprised when I heard myself say it. I hadn't known I liked my father that much.

The chili made me feel warm, but that didn't last long. I had on my coat and my madder sweater and the mittens Miz Liz knitted, but it was really cold. I could feel it. I started to walk all the way home, but I didn't hurry to keep warm. I *wanted* to feel cold.

I walked and walked. Pretty soon my face was stiff and my lips didn't move too well, but I kept on between the houses and the bare trees just walking. The houses get farther apart as you get to the edge of town. My legs were stiff with cold too, but I didn't care. Then there was a cluster of small houses at one place.

As I got nearer a little boy and girl called to me from the porch of one of them and then ran down the walk to me. They had on bright red coats and the little girl had a hood on hers.

"Hello," said the little boy. "Don't you want to pet our dog?"

They had a small black dog about four months old at the end of a light rope that must have been about fifteen feet long. He ran up to me and tried to lick my face when I bent over, and he twisted and squirmed with delight as I took off my right mitten and stroked him with fingers that were almost numb. His coat was soft and tightly curled like the Persian lamb coat one of my aunts has.

"He's a nice dog," I said. "What's his name?"

" 'Doggie'," said the little girl proudly. The little boy smiled all over, and the dog wriggled and raced and got the rope all twisted around the boy.

"Is that all?"

"Well, he isn't a kitty, is he?" the little girl said.

"It's a good name," I said. "Is he a spaniel?"

The little boy had got himself untwisted now. "He's a poodle terrier," he said. "She wanted a poodle and I wanted a terrier so our father gave us one that's both."

Then all three of them ran back the way they'd come, and two of them waved to me from the porch as I started off again.

I felt warm now. It was a good little spaniel, and I like kids who want to share what they like best.

Somehow they gave me an idea. As soon as I got home I went straight to the library and turned on the ceiling light because the lamp on the desk is broken. The room seemed very empty, and the books looked as cold and lonely as I'd felt before I'd met the little boy and girl and their "poodle terrier."

I knew what I wanted. I opened the top drawer of the desk, but they weren't in there. I opened two more drawers but all they had in them were papers. In the next drawer I found what I was looking for. It was one of those leather cases and there were eyeglasses in it. I looked through them and everything was blurred and my eyes watered so I knew they were all right because that's the way people's glasses are supposed to be. Probably they were old ones, but they'd be better than having none.

I was warm now. I was even sweating because I had not stopped to take off my sheepskin. I put the glasses carefully in its inside pocket. Then I hurried out to the barn for my new bike. That bike can go, and I pumped hard. The wind was like ice and my eyes watered again. Part way is downhill so it didn't take me too long to get back to the hospital. I didn't stop at the desk because they always tell you you can't do what you want to do. I was so cold I walked the way an icicle would walk if it could as I hurried to my father's room. I had a hard job getting the glasses out of my inside pocket because my hands were so cold, but I did and left them on the bed table where he could find them and tiptoed out.

It was harder going home and even colder and getting dark. I didn't push so hard but I was glad to get off that bike and into the house.

"Where you been?" asked Miz Liz.

"I went for a ride on my new bike," I said.

"Suppose that's what it's for," she said.

We had pork chops and roast potatoes and mince pie. In winter it isn't worth eating any other kind of pie except maybe sweet potato. Before I went to sleep that night I thought about the little boy and girl and their dog, and it made me feel good all over again.

When I went to see my father the next day he seemed a little stronger. He said I'd been wrong about his eyeglasses. Somebody had found them and brought them to his room. I said I was glad. He had the glasses on and his eyes were clear as he looked at me through them, and I felt good about that too.

"You and Miz Liz getting along all right?"

"We always do."

"That's good," he said and took off his glasses and reached out and put them carefully on the table and fell asleep again.

I went to see my father every day after school. It gave me something to do. I did something else. I wore the wrist compass he had brought me from San Francisco. I even kept it on at night. My father had given it to me so I thought it might help him somehow.

Other people were allowed to see him for a few minutes now. A man came one time from the college and another time two women, but he doesn't pay much attention to most people so there weren't too many others. There were cards, though, which he didn't look at, and flowers in vases and pots. I didn't think too much of them. They were just from florists.

My uncle checked on my father a couple of times a day. He was in the hospital most of the time just then because he had a lot of operations to do. I kept asking him if I could go to the farm, and Saturday morning he said he was going out for a couple of hours to see to things and I could go if I wanted. When we got there I hurried across the fields with my .22.

82

There's nothing says that mistletoe is only good at Christmas, and I was glad I'd left some good bunches on the black walnuts. I got two down with just three shots and I took them to the hospital that afternoon. I put them in a jar of water among the other flowers so there would be something real there. My father might never notice but I'd know.

It was that night when I was in my room reading the horse book Miss Susan had given me that the telephone rang. I knew Miz Liz was down cellar getting some muscadine preserve so I answered.

"Oliver, was it in the paper this evening? It will be in the *Courier-Journal* too so please get me twenty-five copies. This morning the ladies elected me president — national president! Isn't that wonderful! I'm sorry I couldn't call before but we've been *so* busy. Be sure to get the papers. Fifty might be better." It was my mother, and she was talking fast and loud.

"This isn't Oliver," I said. "He isn't home."

My mother's voice changed. "Vergil, are you listening in on the line again? Get me Hamilton then right away."

"He isn't here either."

"He isn't? Then where is he?"

"In Europe, I guess."

"Vergil, don't you dare talk back to your mother! Be sure to tell them what I've told you and that I can't possibly be home for another two weeks. There is so much to do. My inauguration will be in Washington next week. I must get new clothes. Then I must preside at a board meeting in Cleveland. Do you understand?"

I could hear other women's voices in the background but not what they were saying.

"Congratulations," I said.

"Never mind that," said my mother. "Just tell your father and Hamilton what I've told you. I know they will be delighted. I don't think I'll have time to call again." Then her voice changed again so I suppose some of the other women could hear. "Thank you, darling, and be a good boy till Mummy comes home, won't you. Goodbye."

I said goodbye too but she'd hung up by that time. What was she president of now I wondered. I guessed it was the Ladies Union or something like that.

"Who was that?" asked Miz Liz, coming up from the cellar.

"Nobody," I said, but then I told her.

"Keep it to ourselves a while," Miz Liz said. "Tell your father when he gets better."

There were no books in my father's room at the hospital, not even newspapers or magazines, but he never reads them anyway. I knew that if I were in the hospital I'd want Cicero and my .22 so I knew he must miss his books. I didn't know which ones of his to take him so I took him my horse book. I knew most of it by heart now.

My father was sitting in a chair in his bathrobe with a blanket over his knees when I handed it to him.

"What's this?" he said and looked at the cover and turned over some of the pages.

"It's a book," I said.

"I thought it was the Falls of the Ohio," he said, so I knew he was feeling a little better. "Your favorite?" He gestured at me with the book.

"Right now," I said.

"Getting along all right in school?"

"The principal understands boys," I said.

That made him laugh and it was the first time I'd heard him laugh since that night, and I wished I could think of something more to make him laugh but I couldn't.

12

MY UNCLE CALLED ME INTO MY FATHER'S LIBRARY A few nights later. He took my father's chair behind the big desk and I sat in one facing him.

"Well, doctor," he said, "what do you think?"

"I think he wants to come home."

"Patient beginning to fret. That's a good sign, isn't it?"

"He just wants to be back to himself again."

"He's been away from himself longer than he knows, but that's another thing. Shall we release him?"

"What do *you* think?"

"You're the doctor. You were called in first. I've just been consulting on this case."

"I think we should let him out."

"We'll do it tomorrow," my uncle decided.

A nurse took my father down to the side entrance of the hospital in a wheel chair. My uncle's big car was waiting, and he helped my father into the back seat and got in after him. Miss Susan was driving. They both helped my father up the front steps and then up to his big bedroom at the front of the house that Miz Liz had all ready for him. The bed was turned back, and the thermometer was in a glass and his pills were beside it on the table.

My father didn't want to but Uncle Henry ordered him into bed to rest after the excitement of coming home. He said he could get up and walk around the room a little in the morning. Then my uncle left but Miss Susan didn't. Her substitute was going to help him in the office and Miss Susan was going to stay with us to look after my father for a week or two. Uncle Henry said she was the best nurse in Kentucky even if she did come from Georgia.

He had told her everything to do, and Miz Liz had a room all ready for her right next to my father's. Uncle Henry told Miz Liz something too before he left.

"You know how dogs crawl under the barn if they feel ill and stay there until they feel better? That's what I want him to do. Let him stay under the barn as long as he likes and come out when he likes. I don't want him upset."

"Isn't nobody here going to upset him. You know that," Miz Liz said. "Now you go on about your business and tell things to people don't know them in the first place."

My uncle laughed and pretty soon I heard him drive away fast.

Something had been bothering me and I hadn't been able to figure out what it was. Something was different. Suddenly as I was going downstairs after watching them put my father to bed I knew what it was. He didn't squint so much any more.

Miz Liz must have known what I was thinking about the way she does sometimes. "Leastways," she said to Miss Susan while we were all eating in the kitchen that night, "his eyes have had a rest."

It seems funny somebody has to get sick before it happens but now Miz Liz and Miss Susan in her white nurse's dress and I had a good time. We all felt better because my father was home and because Uncle Henry said he would be all right if we took care of him and he took care of himself. He couldn't come downstairs, but he could move around up there when he wanted to, and if he didn't want to, he didn't have to. It was fun having Miss Susan eat with Miz Liz and me. They like each other and they talked a lot about all kinds of things and I listened. It's interesting to watch other people, especially if they don't know you're doing it.

My father didn't look so white and scared and kind of surprised now. I began to tell him things like what I did in school that day and how I was going to train Stethoscope and things I saw down by the river. You can't just sit and stare at people. You have to say something. I don't know whether my father listened or not. You can hardly ever tell.

Uncle Henry didn't stay at the house any but he came every day, and one afternoon I heard him telling my father things. "You have indefinite sick leave from the college so you have nothing to worry about there. Everything is under control in the house so you have nothing to worry about here. I envy you. Just poke around a while. When spring comes get outdoors and stay there. Remember this could happen again and it would be worse the next time."

My father didn't answer. I didn't hear him anyway. Probably he just made a face. One day when I couldn't think of anything else I asked him if he wanted me to bring my skeleton up to look at. He said not to bother because he had a skeleton, and he pointed to himself. He was really thin. Miz Liz kept trying to stuff him but he wouldn't eat much. He doesn't even when he's well.

Probably you've noticed that good things don't last forever. Cicero and I had just come home from school and I was having milk and a big piece of chocolate cake in the kitchen with Miz Liz when a taxicab swung into the drive. I think we both knew right off what it was and had been afraid so we didn't move for a minute. We just sat there and waited.

My mother swept into the front hall all smiles and talking loudly and looking happy and angry at the same time.

"Pay the cabman, somebody! He's bringing in my bags. Oliver, where are you? I fully expected that after all this time that you would meet me at the airport. I'm worn out. Vergil, where's your father?"

"He's been sick," I said.

"Sick! Why wasn't I notified?"

"No need to worry you, you being so busy," said Miz Liz.

Just then Miss Susan started down the stairs carrying a tray.

"Who is this?"

"It's Miss Susan," I said.

"Who? Oh, Dr. Trewbridge's receptionist. I didn't recognize you in your uniform. Then Dr. Trewbridge is here? Does Mr. Trewbridge have influenza? Everyone in Baltimore and Cleveland seemed to be coming down with influenza. It's a wonder I didn't catch it with all the running around I've been doing."

"Uncle Henry isn't here and Father doesn't have the flu," I said.

"Then I don't understand. Put them all right down there," she told the cabman. "Vergil, take them to my room and be careful not to bang against things. Has anybody kept a list of my phone calls? Where is Hamilton?"

I carried up the bags and cases two at a time. I made three trips and didn't scratch any of the doors or the furniture. Then I got Cicero and went out the back. We walked all the way down to the river and watched it going by. It was high because we'd had lots more rain and there were some branches and a couple of boards floating in it but nothing I wanted. I looked around for a muskrat but I didn't see one. I didn't see anything but the dark water rushing, the brown leaves still on the oaks, and the gray sky. I thought a beech looked a lot like my skeleton only bigger, of course.

I didn't want to go back to the house so I walked around and kicked things and threw some sticks for Cicero to fetch. I saw a few birds because there are always birds in Kentucky, but they weren't quail or any other bird I was interested in. I thought maybe I ought to go to my room and do some homework, but I didn't want to do that and I didn't want to ride my bike.

When I went back in Miz Liz shook her head and pointed upstairs so I knew my mother was up talking to my father. There was no sound from up there. You can't hear people anyway unless they are talking loudly and my father never does. My mother does but not when she doesn't want to.

I didn't want to hear even if I could so I went out again and went around front and kicked one of the pillars. Cicero wanted to play again. I told him I couldn't be playing all the time and walked out the drive and down the road and he came to heel. That's what he does when he thinks things are serious to show he can be serious too.

A couple of cars went by. It was almost dark so they had their headlights on, but you can never be sure they see you, so Cicero and I jumped down into the ditch at the side of the road and watched them pass. I wondered who was in the cars and where they were going. Then I wondered why people are always going places all the time. Nobody stays still long. It was a good dry ditch with high dead weeds in it. They rustled and smelled like poor hay. I'd never feed Stethoscope stuff like that. We stayed some more and watched a few more cars and one farm truck go by. Then we went back.

My father had been going to come down to dinner for the first time that night. Miz Liz had cooked some of the things he likes best, and Miss Susan had helped her set the table with a white linen cloth and candles and the heavy silver. I wondered whether my father would come now but he did, and my mother thought the table had been set for her homecoming and was pleased.

Uncle Henry was there too. He had not planned to come but Miss Susan had telephoned him that my mother was home. Then Miss Susan suddenly remembered that she had things to attend to at the place where she lives so she couldn't stay, and she took her bag with her when she went.

So that my mother wouldn't worry, as soon as we were seated my Uncle Henry said, "Oliver has done very well, better than I expected."

"Much better, I'm sure," my mother said. "I still think it strange I was not notified. Perhaps it was hard to reach me by telephone but certainly you could have reached one of my assistants."

I was surprised. I didn't know she had any assistants. "What do they assist you to do?" I asked. My mother did not answer me and no one else did.

"I find it even stranger," said my mother, "that during my absence my son has been driven from his home."

"Nobody druv him," said Miz Liz. She was serving the soup.

"Strangest of all," said my mother, "is that I cannot leave home for a few days to do my little part in bettering social conditions without coming home to find a strange woman in my house."

I wanted to help smooth things out so I said, "Miss Susan's not a stranger. You know her."

"I certainly do!"

My uncle looked really angry. "Like all of us, Sybil, you are only a biological accident, but must you insist on being a catastrophe?"

"No, thank you, Miz Liz," I heard my father say when she started to serve him his soup.

"Biological accident! Biological accident! Nice talk before an innocent young boy! For too long we women have been supine and acquiescent. For too long. . ." It sounded as if my mother had memorized it. I think it is what she says in some of her speeches. She went on with more stuff like that.

All of a sudden I saw something. I think I'd sort of known it for a long time, but I didn't know I knew it until right then. I think my mother takes after me sometimes in some ways. When she wants to be liked the most, particularly when she wants my father and my uncle to like her, she goes all thumbs and says things she doesn't mean or says them the wrong way. Maybe my uncle knew it too.

He didn't look angry any more. He put on his most charming smile, the one he uses with difficult patients. "I think I know a real woman when I see one," he said.

My mother, who had been about to go on with her speech, opened her eyes wide, and she almost blushed. "Why, Henry! Why, Henry, thank you!"

My uncle put his charming smile away so he could use it some other time and looked at me.

"Miz Liz, this roast beef is delicious!" my mother cried.

"It's so good to have home cooking again. How I wish you could all have been there, especially Hamilton. We had all worked so hard, and when the votes were counted it was the culmination of all our efforts!"

Miz Liz put more roast beef and another roast potato on my plate.

"Of course, the national president must coordinate the efforts of all our local chapters, and so many of them, poor dears, are so lacking in experience that they need all kinds of advice and counsel. I'm afraid I am faced with a great deal of hard traveling!"

My mother kept on and on and her whole face was shining. No one else said anything. Miz Liz and my uncle and I just ate.

"It's all quite wonderful, Sybil," my father said finally, "and we're all very happy for you."

My mother beamed. She even smiled at me.

My father had eaten part of a hot biscuit but that was all. He didn't look at anybody when he moved a little in his chair and said, "I'm afraid I feel a little tired. If you will all excuse me." His hand trembled a little on the chair when he got up.

"Bring you something to eat later," said Miz Liz.

I got up and went with my father in case he had trouble getting up the stairs without Miss Susan there to help. He didn't go up to his bedroom though. He went to his library and snapped on the wall light. He sat in his chair and I turned on the lamp, which had been repaired.

"So this is where I spend my days," he said.

"Just part. You're at the college a lot."

"Yes, I suppose so."

There were piles of letters on his desk, some of them in the big envelopes that booksellers' catalogues and advertising come in. My father looked at the pile and then he tipped it over. Then he poked at the mess.

"What do you think would happen if I never opened any of these?"

"I don't know," I said.

"Do you suppose the heavens would fall?"

"No."

"Do you think I'd get struck by lightning?"

"Mostly we only get thunderstorms in the summer."

"And this is winter. Exactly. Ask Miz Liz to bring me some soup here, will you. It smelled good."

"It *is* good," I said, and I went to tell Miz Liz.

13

ALL WEEK LONG THE TEACHERS TALKED ABOUT ecology and the environment. They said ecology was a good thing and we should all be in favor of it and take care of the environment. Then on Friday morning the whole school went to the auditorium, and the principal talked some more about the beauties of nature and showed an eight-millimeter color motion picture he took of it when he went to a principals' meeting in Tennessee. The picture wasn't much good, but everyone clapped because we got out of two whole classes.

When we got back to our home room, the teacher was all excited and said we were going to take part in an important project. First we would sign a paper saying we would never burn leaves and pollute the air or throw things into the water and pollute the water and use chemicals and pollute the earth and kill the bugs because they maintain the balance of nature. And we were all in favor of the balance of nature, weren't we? She knew our class was going to sign 100 percent the way the other classes were doing. Then the whole school was going to march to city hall in favor of ecology.

The whole thing made me sick. Our family's always taken care of the land, the trees, the streams and the animals. We take care of the land just the way my uncle takes care of the people on it. It's nothing new with us, and we know how to do it.

Now some people were acting as if caring for the earth and things that grow on it were something they'd just discovered or invented, and making up big words like "ecology" and talking as loud as they could about things most of them don't know anything about. That's what I don't like — a lot of noisy people pushing their way into good things. All they ever do except talk is bungle around and destroy what is good. I don't let just anybody pat Cicero. He wouldn't let them anyway. It was like that too, and that's how we feel.

The teacher passed the paper around, and the kids began to sign. When it came to me, I didn't sign it but passed it along. In the first place I don't like to sign anything. If you're not careful, you can find you've signed away your dog or your grandfather if you have one, which I don't.

In the second place I knew the principal didn't know a Tennessee Walking Horse from a mule, and the teacher couldn't tell a mockingbird from a cottonwood. I had a lot of other reasons, so I didn't sign.

When the teacher got the paper back she was as pleased as anything until she counted the names and then counted us.

"Somebody forgot to sign," she said. "Who forgot to sign?"

Nobody raised his hand and I didn't.

"Somebody didn't sign," she said.

I raised my hand then. "I didn't forget to sign," I said. "I just didn't."

"Why, Vergil Trewbridge! You of all the boys in this class! I'm sure you want to sign. Don't you have a pen?"

"I have a pen," I said, "but I'm not signing."

The teacher looked all bothered. "But you *must* be in favor of ecology!"

"I like to burn leaves," I said. "I like the smell and the potash is good for the soil. Not all the leaves, of course. People shouldn't rake around their shrubs. The leaves are a natural mulch and turn into good compost. Look in the woods and you'll see. The soil is black. Sometimes it's a little sour and you have to use lime, but it's good soil."

94

"Oh, if that's all," said the teacher. She looked relieved.

"The Indians used to burn the fields and woods in the spring," I said. "They got rid of the dead grass and weeds and the underbrush that way so the new growth could start and the brush wouldn't choke the trees."

"Now he thinks he's an Indian!" said Johnny Pratt.

"Whoo-whoo-whoop!" said Mike Steinbeck so the girls would laugh, and they did.

"That was a long time ago," the teacher said. "Smoke pollutes the air we all breathe."

"Breathing pollutes it worse," I said. "People should stop breathing."

"That will be about enough, Vergil Trewbridge," the teacher said.

"But there's more," I said. "You have to use chemical sprays if you want the trees to fruit. We wouldn't have any apples if we let the bugs eat the leaves and buds or pears or plums or peaches either."

"One more word, Vergil, and I shall be forced to send you to the principal. You should be ashamed of yourself. Don't you want our class to be 100 percent?"

That's another thing I'm against, 100 percent. It means everybody thinks the same, which isn't possible, or that nobody is thinking at all, which is more likely. I've heard my father say that. So I said, "No."

That was the one more word so the teacher told me to leave the room and to go the principal's office. The class laughed when I went out the door, and I heard one girl say now they were 100 percent to show she could count.

"Well, well, what have we here?" the principal said when I went into his office.

"I'm against ecology," I said.

He smiled all over at me and oiled his voice. "I'm sure you're not. It just hasn't been properly explained to you. You don't know quite what it is. Isn't that it?"

"I know what it is," I said.

"Oh! So you just felt like being a little rebellious today?

95

You didn't like your lunch or something went a little wrong on the way to school. I understand boys, you know."

I didn't say anything. I looked out the window and wished I were outside.

"I used to be a boy myself," the principal said and laughed and laughed. I just looked at him. Probably he didn't even know how many eggs a hen pheasant sets on. He thought I didn't know it was a joke so he said it again. "I was a boy once."

You have to be polite and say something, so I said, "When?"

He didn't like that and didn't tell me when. He stopped laughing and looked stern. That's the way he does.

"Don't you want to be 100 percent?"

I shook my head.

"This is more serious than you realize, Vergil," he said. "Are you sure you don't want to sign and take your position as a stalwart in the school community?"

"I'm sure," I said.

"That is most unfortunate. As past president and honorary chairman of the P.T.A. your good mother is very much in favor of this drive. In fact, she is one of the moving spirits behind it."

I hadn't known that. If I had known, I might have signed and let it go even if it was a lie.

"I feel it my duty to telephone her."

I couldn't give in now. Besides, I knew my mother was in Charleston to talk to the chapter of the Ladies Union there, and they were having a big dinner in her honor and it was all going to be on local television.

"Go ahead," I said.

The principal reached for his telephone. He moved slowly to see if I wouldn't ask to be forgiven and promise to be a good boy. He kept watching me. I watched him back. My father wouldn't answer his telephone, and Miz Liz had gone shopping. He wouldn't get any answer. He didn't either, and it made him angry.

"You may go now," he said sharply.

I think he meant I could go back to my class, but I decided he meant I could go home, and I went.

Mr. Kinney knows more ecology in the little finger of his right hand that is crooked, where he broke it when he was young and it was never set, than they do with all their yapping heads. Cicero and Stethoscope and their ancestors have been practicing it for a long time. Cicero helps the balance of nature by killing rabbits, and he would kill a cat if he could catch one. Stethoscope does it just by eating grass. They don't have projects about it and get a lot of other dogs and horses out marching and shouting. You get a deer loose in your vegetable garden and he'll show you about the balance of nature!

Of course, I'm for ecology. I always have been. I didn't exactly lie when I told the principal I was against it because it's no use trying to explain some things to some people. I'm against that word all right but I can't help being for what is in my blood and my bones just the way it is in my father's and my uncle's and Mr. Kinney's.

My mother would come home after a while, and the principal would keep calling until he reached her. He likes to telephone almost as much as she does, and they both talk about 100 percent all the time. Things didn't look so good again, but there wasn't anything I could do about it now. I went and had my chili, but I was sort of nervous and put too much salt and pepper on my French fries, and they made me cough.

"You got the heaves," Tony said and brought me a glass of water.

I drank it quickly and shook my head. "It's not the heaves," I told him when I could speak. "It's stupid people."

"Git coughin' from them you never stop," he said. "More of 'em every day includin' holidays."

I walked all the way home going as slowly as I could so it would not look as if I'd left school early. When I got there my father was walking around and around the drive. He does it every afternoon now even when it rains. He puts on his raincoat and an old hat. He saw me before I got there and waved so I walked around with him. He didn't say much, and I didn't tell him what had happened in school because I didn't want to worry him. It wasn't raining this day but it was mild, and there was some pale sun. We stood in a patch of it near the road and looked back at the house.

My father said it needed painting but he hadn't realized it before. I said I could paint the low parts and he could paint the high parts because he's taller. Then if we got some ladders and a scaffold we could reach all the way to the tops of the pillars and up to the eaves. He said we'd better let regular painters do it.

In school they say people shouldn't cut down trees. Well, our house is made of wood and most houses are, and the only way I know to get wood is to chop down trees, so what are they talking about? Then the ecology people go and cut down millions and millions of Christmas trees, and they think that's fine. We plant trees all the time at the farm and around the house too. That's what I was thinking about, but I didn't say anything.

My father seemed glad to be out. He looked glad, and he looked well. I thought he looked even better than before he fell in the library, but I didn't say anything about that either. People are always asking people how they feel, especially if they have been sick, and they get tired of it.

When we went in, I told Miz Liz I didn't want anything to eat, and she knew why, but she didn't say anything about the chili and French fries in front of my father. Then my father went to his library, and I went to my room.

The first thing I did was open the closet door and look at my skeleton. I looked at him a long time. I suppose he was hanged because he didn't agree with everyone and wasn't one hundred percent. I felt sorry for him and for me too.

14

MY MOTHER WAS ALL EXCITED WHEN SHE CAME home. They'd made a big fuss over her in Charleston and she said they were making great progress there. By the time they had their regional meeting in Knoxville the Ladies Union would be more powerful and effective under her leadership than ever. I heard her telling my father.

At school hardly anyone spoke to me but they looked at me. The teacher was very polite, but she never called on me and I never raise my hand to answer questions. I didn't see the principal at all. They were making a lot of plans about ecology and posters and slogans and having competitions for the best but I was left out of everything to show me I didn't matter.

I kept waiting for my mother to send for me but I think she was so busy telephoning for a couple of days that the principal couldn't reach her. Then he did and it was just about what I expected.

"Evidently you care nothing at all about your father," she said.

I didn't say anything.

"You are trying your best to give him another heart attack."

"No, I'm not," I said.

"I never knew what brought on the first, but I have suspected all along it was something you did."

I didn't answer that either.

"It's very clear now that you won't be satisfied until you make his last days unhappy," she said.

I knew they weren't his last days. My uncle had told me.

"Of course, you have never cared anything at all about me."

"Yes, I do," I said then and it was true. I like my mother better than Margaret Hobart's mother and the other women who come to the house.

"The principal tells me — he has been *forced* to tell me — of your misbehavior. I am hardly surprised you took advantage of my absence but I cannot understand your lack of interest in the environment. Don't you care anything about other people?"

"Not much," I said, "but I'll leave them alone if they leave me alone."

My mother looked helpless. "Your brother Hamilton cares for all the world and he loves nature."

"I know he does," I said. "He sings at it and plays his guitar at it."

My mother sighed. "If only Hamilton were home to help me with my burdens," she said. "If you could only understand how badly your principal feels — and he understands boys — that you are not 100 percent. If you knew how badly *I* feel, but, of course, that doesn't matter to you!"

I could see my mother was getting stuck so I tried to help her. "Don't feel badly," I said.

"Then you *will* change your mind and take part in this splendid endeavor to help the human race? That's what mother is trying to do all the time."

You can't keep fighting always but at least you don't have to say anything. You can keep it to yourself. I wasn't going to change, but I didn't have to say so. Besides, my mother looked so hopeful.

"Maybe," I said.

Her face lighted up the way it does when she is on the platform and people are clapping.

"I knew I could make you see. I understand boys too. After all, I'm a mother."

"I guess so," I said.

She changed then. "You can see how busy mother is, can't you? Now run along and play with your little dog."

"All right," I said.

So I didn't do anything and the school went ahead with its ecology and they had their parade, but I didn't go. I went out to the farm with my uncle and tied a long rope on Stethoscope's halter and showed him how to run around and around in the paddock at the end of the rope. Once he understood, he loved it and we had a good time. My uncle watched and said I was doing all right and I forgot all about ecology.

In a couple of weeks the school forgot all about ecology too and forgot I'd been a villain again. You can always depend on that. Things get forgotten and probably it's a good thing. I bet you can't even remember what you ate for breakfast yesterday.

Some horses will come when you whistle. I've seen that in the movies and on television. I don't have to whistle for Stethoscope. Unless he's busy swishing his tail at a fly or running a race with himself or rolling in a mud puddle or wants to show me how he can almost turn a somersault, he comes as soon as he sees me. He wants to be petted.

Scalpel watches and looks bored or else he gets jealous and nips at Stethoscope or tries to kick him, not hard though. He isn't, but Scalpel thinks he's Stethoscope's father and tries to tell him what to do. Stethoscope thinks so too except when he doesn't want to. People are a lot like animals. Some people think it is the other way around and animals are like people, but it isn't.

My uncle looked at me one day. "Don't grow any more," he said. "You're about the right weight for a jockey now. You're a little taller than most of them but that's not bad. Live weight is better than dead lead."

I want to grow some more. I want to be as tall as he is and my father is but not right away. I hoped I wouldn't grow any more until Stethoscope is four years old. There's a reason for that.

"Had the saddle on him yet?" my uncle asked.

"No, but I've had the bridle on him twice and left it on him in his stall for an hour. He likes it. He thinks he's all dressed up. He tries to bite the bit though."

"He would. Just take your time. Let him think he thought it all up by himself."

You learn a lot being a doctor and then forget where you learned it. What my uncle told me to do is what he does with people. He knows it is the same with horses and I know he's right. He told me to put a little salt and flaxseed in with Stethoscope's crushed oats. I did and he liked it.

First I showed it to him and then I put the saddle on Stethoscope in his stall the very next week. He kept turning his head to see what I was doing and after I got it on practically turned himself inside out to look. He was just showing off. He knew what it was and he thought it was fun. He began stepping around the box stall to show how handsome he is.

I didn't tell anyone but I'd been on his back lots of times. What I do is shut Scalpel in the paddock so he won't bother us and take Stethoscope away out in the pasture out of sight of the house and ride him bareback with just his halter. At first he was skittish because he didn't know what I wanted. Then he understood and didn't object. He knows I can't keep up with him running or walking so he decided he might just as well take me along with him. There were things he wanted to show me out there and, of course, we went where he wanted to go because I couldn't guide him with just the halter.

Sometimes he walked and sometimes he trotted or cantered and I jolted up and down on his backbone. A few times he galloped, but I didn't. I fell off. I fell off so hard a time or two that I got some good bumps and bruises, and once I thought I'd cracked parts of me that I don't want cracked, but

I didn't. Stethoscope would keep on going full speed but then he'd brake or circle back to see what in the world had happened to me. The worst time I had to pull myself back up with his halter rope and he helped. I didn't mount again that time either. I walked back using him as a big crutch but by the time we reached the stable I wasn't dizzy.

That night Miz Liz demanded to know how I could get so dirty and how I'd torn my shirt and the old windbreaker I was wearing. I tried to stand up straight and not show how stiff and sore I was but she saw and thought I'd fallen off my ten-speed.

"Those new-fangled bicycles!" she said. "What's a body need all those speeds for? Can't go more'n one at a time."

"I did," I said. I meant I went half a dozen when I fell off Stethoscope and not all of them the same way.

The next time I put Stethoscope's bridle on when we went for a bareback ride. He wasn't too happy about that. He thought I was making him go one way when he wanted to go another so he set his feet and wouldn't go anywhere at all. That is until he saw Cicero chasing a rabbit across the fields and wanted to know what he was doing. He got the bit in his teeth and we all went after that rabbit, me hanging to the reins and Stethoscope's mane and about everything but his tail.

There wasn't any rabbit so Stethoscope started playing tag with Cicero the way they do and I had to whether I wanted to or not until I fell off again. This time I landed in a patch of old burdock and beggars' lice and got scratched and stung and scraped my face. It took a half hour to get the burrs and stickers off me and out of me. I put some of the petroleum jelly in the tack room on my face before I went home but it was swollen and I had a black eye.

Of course, I had to run into my mother coming home from somewhere.

"You've been fighting at school again!"

"No, ma'am."

I was saved by the bell, the way people say. I really was. Her telephone rang and she hurried up the stairs.

I don't know who it was but I heard her say, "Of course, it's doubly hard for me with Oliver in his condition. People make such a fuss over heart attacks these days. Of course, they are becoming quite fashionable. I don't know why I don't have one myself. Thursday? No, Thursday would be impossible; Friday too. Perhaps some day next week before I go to Detroit. Perhaps . . ."

It just happened that my father heard her too. He goes to the college a few hours most days now. He'd just come home too and was standing in the hall.

"I wasn't fighting, really I wasn't," I said.

"What? Oh, I see."

What I saw was that he didn't see anything just then so I went to take a hot shower and patch myself and put on clean clothes before anybody asked me any more questions. I'd torn my sweater too. Well, it was my old gray one that was already torn so I just hid it. I was glad I'd not been wearing my madder red. I take good care of it and only wear it when I want to feel good.

I was so busy with Stethoscope that I really didn't have time for school now. I went every day because that's what you're supposed to do and it gets to be a habit, but I sat in class thinking about my mother and father and my uncle and Miss Susan but mostly about Stethoscope and what to do next.

The hard thing is to get a colt to do what you want him to do and not what he wants. I kept telling him and he listened and I tried to show him. He knew well enough and he really wanted to do what I told him, but he had to show me that he was independent and could do things he wished sometimes. I said that people are like horses and dogs — only not as decent.

Sometimes I didn't wait for my uncle or Miss Susan to drive me to the farm. I went on my bike. It was pretty far and sometimes I got winded, but you always get a second wind if you wait a minute. I knew my uncle was watching me with Stethoscope though he didn't want me to know and didn't go out with me to the pasture or even to the paddock much. Most of the time, of course, he wasn't there but in town setting bones or taking out appendixes or putting stitches in people and things like that.

I planned it all very carefully and explained it to him for three days before I put both the saddle and bridle on Stethoscope and took him out to the end of the pasture and mounted. When I pulled his head to the right and pressed my right knee into his shoulder he turned to the left.

"No!" I said. "No, no, no, no!"

He cocked an ear and turned to see me, then went straight ahead.

So we tried it again and he did the same thing again. Either it was just to show me or he likes to hear me say, "No, no, no, no!"

That's the way it went for a few times. Then all of a sudden Stethoscope decided to do it my way. I had only to pull the rein a little and just touch him with my knee and he did just what I wanted. He was as pleased with himself as he had been when he was doing things his way. He was like Cicero when he decides to be on his best behavior.

Now it was really fun. We went for long rides, trotting and galloping through the pasture and even off over the fields toward the woods. Stethoscope had learned to jump from Scalpel. One day when I wasn't expecting it he leaped high over a gate tossing me high into the air. I landed on my shoulder and felt it bend and kind of squeal but it didn't break.

That meant I had to put off what I had planned for another week until my shoulder got so it didn't hurt. Then I waited for my father outside about the time I know he comes home. My uncle lets him drive now if he doesn't go too far. I opened the car door and he got out. It was a pretty day and the radio said that the next day, which was Saturday, would be pretty too.

"Don't you ever go out to Uncle Henry's farm?" I asked him as we were walking to the house.

"I've not been there in, why, it must be two years almost."

"Will you drive me out tomorrow? Uncle Henry is going to be there and he told you you should be outdoors. I heard him."

My father looked down at me and smiled. "Why not?" he said quickly. I knew he would do it then. He never goes back on his word.

Uncle Henry looked surprised when my father and I walked into the farmhouse dining room. He and Mr. and Mrs. Kinney were just finishing lunch.

"Came by formal invitation," my father said. "How's the famous colt?"

"Don't know," said my uncle. "That's up to Verge. Let's go see."

We all went to the stable. I tried hard not to hurry ahead of them. When we got there my father said Stethoscope looked well formed and sound. He'd grown and he was losing his winter coat. I knew, for I'd brushed a lot of hair out of him.

"Stand still for a saddle yet?" my father asked.

"Will he, Verge?"

I didn't answer. I had everything ready and I just went into the stall and put Stethoscope's bridle on him and then his saddle and led him out.

My father looked surprised now. My uncle's eyes were narrow as he watched my father as well as the colt and me. I led Stethoscope to the paddock, mounted at the gate, and began to walk him around the little track. Then I let him trot. We went around and around, Stethoscope moving as smooth as silk.

"Hands just a little higher! Hold them firm! Tighten your knees a little!"

It was my father and his face was all lighted. I did as he said and it felt better. Then I felt Stethoscope's muscles tighten and we flew through the open gate and across the pasture. He really went, and I never felt better in my life than I did with Stethoscope streaking across the land and the wind cutting my face and his hooves thudding into the earth and my father and my uncle watching. I slowed Stethoscope, turned, and we raced back to the paddock.

Stethoscope wasn't even breathing hard when I slid off the saddle and landed at my father's feet, but I was.

"Who trained him?" he asked as he stroked the colt's neck.

"Nobody," I said. "He trained himself. I helped him."

My father turned to my uncle. "About fourteen hands?"

"About, but he'll go fifteen."

"Good shoulders," my father said. He didn't look at me at all, just at Stethoscope. My uncle had been right. My father did know about horses.

There are times when you feel good. There are not so many times when you feel so much better than that that you don't know what to do. This was one of them. I wanted to shout and jump and do cartwheels but I didn't. I jumped back on Stethoscope and we rode some more, just loping in the paddock.

Uncle Henry and my father watched closely. Except that my father's hair is gray and he wears glasses, they look much the same. What they were talking about I didn't know, and I was so busy handling Stethoscope and so happy and trying not to show how happy I was that I didn't care.

"Has a good stride," my father said as he led Stethoscope back to the stable.

"Not much power though," my uncle said.

"He may have."

"Not for racing. Just a fine Thoroughbred."

"I'm glad we have one Kentucky thoroughbred in the family," said my father.

"We *have* one," my uncle said.

"I thought Scalpel was a Thoroughbred too," I said. Probably they didn't hear me because neither of them answered.

My father helped me unsaddle Stethoscope and rub him down. He knew just what to do. Then he gave him a slap on the rump and Stethoscope leaped happily as we let him out to pasture.

We stayed at the farm all afternoon. Fluffy clouds rolled across the bluest blue sky. You could smell spring coming. It was just waiting to pounce. My father, my uncle and I walked and walked over the fields and hills and down by the branch, which was swollen with winter rains. My father knew every foot of the place. He missed a big elm that had come down in a storm, but he found a sassafrass and cut some twigs and we all chewed them as we walked.

Suddenly my uncle stopped. "That's enough."

"Enough what?" said my father.

"Walking for you for one day."

"I feel fine."

"And Verge and I intend to keep you that way. Back to the house."

So we went back and my uncle and my father talked and talked as if they hadn't seen each other in a long time. After a while I went out and when I got far enough away from the house and knew they couldn't hear me or see me I ran and shouted and jumped and ran till I was out of breath. I wanted to get home to tell Cicero.

One day the middle of the next week when I came home from school there were new cardboard boxes on my bed and I wondered what was in them. I untied the biggest, and it was a pair of tan whipcord jodhpurs with suede leather patches inside the knees. I grabbed the next box. It had the kind of short boots with straps you wear with jodhpurs. They were dark brown with a dull shine and their tops soft. In the third box there was a black velvet jockey's cap with a long peak and the inside hard so that in case you fall on your head you won't damage it too much.

I was so excited I couldn't put those clothes on fast enough. I was only half into them when my father said from the doorway, "I got the sizes from Miz Liz. If they don't fit, you can put them on the skeleton. He looks cold enough sometimes." He went and opened the closet door to look at it.

Jodhpurs are better than breeches because you can get in and out of them easier, and that kind of boots is better than riding boots for the same reason. They both fit perfectly. By the time my father turned around I had the things on.

"A car always goes better when it's polished," he said. "Same with a good horse and a good rider."

"I don't have anything to give you," I said.

"You gave me a drink of brandy one night."

"It was two drinks."

"No wonder they had to take me to the hospital! Oh, I forgot on Saturday. Shorten your stirrups one notch. When you get used to that, shorten them one more."

"I will."

Then he went away. There's a mirror in my room and another in the bathroom but they're short. I had to stand on a stool and keep twisting to see all of me. I put the cap on square, then I tipped it to one side and then the other. Then I put it back square again the way it's supposed to be.

I ran to show Miz Liz. "My!" she said. "My!"

I walked into the other rooms and all through the house downstairs. There's a big mirror in the drawing room so now I got a good look. I went all over, even into rooms I don't often go just to hear the sound of my boots on the floor. They were as soft as slippers to my feet. Now I knew the way Margaret Hobart felt about her evening dress at Christmas. I went and put on my madder sweater and showed Miz Liz how good it looked with my riding clothes.

"Horse won't know you," she said.

My mother was going to be home and it was one of those nights Miz Liz said we had to eat in the dining room like civilized people. For once I was glad because I wanted my mother to see me in my jodhpurs and boots.

She saw me all right. She took one look and said, "Vergil, go immediately and change your clothes. I won't have people improperly dressed at my dinner table."

"Verge will remain as he is," said my father, and his voice was hard. "He has my permission."

"Well! Miz Liz, this soup is cold, and I do wish you would not insist on putting okra into everything. It's not done in New York or Boston."

"'s done here," said Miz Liz.

She didn't say the soup was hot enough to burn your tongue. She let my mother find that out and she did.

15

THE NEWSPAPER SAID MY MOTHER HAD BEEN invited to an important conference in Washington along with the leaders of other national organizations. It said that recognition of her contributions was an honor for our town and that it looked forward to even greater things from her at the conference. She was to leave immediately and not return until the conference had reached its objectives.

He almost never does so I was surprised when my father came into the kitchen just as Miz Liz and I were sitting down to breakfast. He was all shaved and dressed.

"Smelled the bacon and coffee," he told Miz Liz. "I'm as hungry as a horse — a Thoroughbred, of course." Going to the farm had waked my father up. He looked alive and glad to be alive.

"That's more like it," said Miz Liz. She poured a cup of coffee for him and put his eggs into boiling water because that's the way he eats them.

"Saw some buds on the maples," my father told me while she was doing that. "It's going to be spring and I haven't seen spring in years."

"It's been here every year," I said.

"It has? I didn't notice. Do you think we ought to go and see it come?"

"I always do," I said.

"Yes, but the place I mean is down in the Gap and at the Falls."

I opened my eyes when he said that.

"Do you think you could tear yourself away from school for a few days?" he asked me.

I swallowed the piece of toast I was eating so fast I almost choked. I had to take a swallow of cocoa before I could say that I thought maybe I could.

I didn't know he knew my mother was in Washington because he doesn't read the paper, but he did know because the next thing he said was, "With Sybil away, Miz Liz, you're coming too. Mrs. Long and the yard man can look after things here."

"Can't go gallivantin' at my age, spring or no spring," said Miz Liz, but her eyes were bright.

"You could wear your fox fur if it doesn't get too warm," I said.

"Maybe even if it does," she said.

Have you ever been down the Cumberland Gap in the early spring when most of the trees are still bare but there are tiny leaves on others and the evergreens are a bright green in the sun? Have you ever seen Cumberland Falls when the snow has just melted up in the hills and the rains have come down hard? It's something. I've heard about Niagara and I've seen pictures of it, but it can't be better than the Cumberland. It roars and splashes and crashes down and the sun shines through the white spray making rainbows.

It was so early in the year that we had everything almost to ourselves, and we looked at the Falls and shouted to make one another hear. We walked around and looked up into the mountains alongside and the valley below where the whirlpools and rapids spill over the rocks. We couldn't get enough of it. We got rooms in the hotel and Miz Liz stayed there because she was tired while my father and I went to Lookout Point on top of the stone cliffs and looked down the gorges to the mountains. They were so far away they looked blue.

We had a good dinner that night and slept hard. Then after breakfast we started out again, just riding and looking. Miz Liz had a wonderful time. She's a little stiff so my father has to help her in and out of the car, but once she's inside she takes charge. She told my father to go slower or faster or to turn here to look for this hill or that house she remembered. She treated him just the way she treats me, as if he weren't any older, and he does what she says to do just the way I do and he likes it.

My father wouldn't tell us where we were going, but about four o'clock that afternoon he pulled up to the big gray inn at Berea. There's a college in Berea, and the buildings and grounds are pretty. Here there were leaves on many of the trees, some a pinkish red, others the palest green. The jonquils and other early bulb flowers were out. Miz Liz knows the names of them all.

That night we had a big dinner, and the waitresses were girls from the college. It was very quiet with just low music and there weren't many people. Miz Liz was all dressed up and she wore earrings. They were not the kind that dangle but little diamond points set right in because her ears were pierced when she was a girl. She said she couldn't wear the hanging ones because her fox scarf might brush them off. She said the dinner was good so it must have been because she usually doesn't think much of other people's cooking.

I had roast turkey with lots of dressing because that was what I wanted, and I ate so many hot biscuits and hush puppies I didn't think I'd want any dessert, but I did when it came because it was deep dish apple pie with heavy cream to pour over it.

There's a skittleboard in the long lobby of the Berea Inn. I'd never seen one before but my father showed me how to play. You spin a top and it knocks down ninepins. He said it is a very old game brought to Kentucky from England a long time ago. He's good at it and I wasn't bad, except once the top got away from me and sailed down the room. It almost hit some people at the desk where the clerk is, but they saw it coming and ducked and just laughed.

We played some more but then a man came who knows my father and he took him to talk to some ladies and another man so Miz Liz and I just sat and watched the people come and go and the students who work at the Inn. After a while my father came for us and we went and talked to the people too. They knew my father had been sick and said it was fortunate my uncle was there. They said one of them owed his life to Dr. Trewbridge and that many other people owed their lives to him too.

One of the men owns a horse farm near Paris so, of course, they talked about the Derby and which horse might win. In Kentucky people talk about the Derby all year long. That made me wonder how Stethoscope was. Then I got sleepy and didn't hear any more.

The next day my father went to see the librarian of the college and Miz Liz and I went for a tour of it with one of the student guides. Miz Liz didn't go all the way, but I did and saw everything, even where they make things like the skittleboard, but they didn't have a skeleton in the museum as good as mine. That night I had roast beef and chocolate layer cake.

None of us really wanted to go home the third day, but we knew we had to. We didn't know anything was wrong until we got to our own house.

As soon as we turned into the curve of our drive I saw the three big black cars like funeral cars in front of the house. There was a state policeman standing there by his motorcycle and another state policeman sitting behind the wheel of the first car.

"What in the world!" gasped my father.

"There's nothing wrong, Oliver! Nothing!" said Miz Liz sharply.

I ran into the house and my father didn't wait for Miz Liz.

One of the state cops touched his cap in half salute to my father as we passed him but he didn't say anything.

There were a lot of people talking in the drawing room, women and men. My mother jumped up to greet us as soon as she saw us. She grabbed me and hugged me hard and there was a bright flash as a photographer took our picture. "One more," he said, kneeling on the floor. "Hold it!" Then he said it was all right and she let me go.

"Oliver!" my mother cried and kissed my father. Then she began to introduce him around.

"The Honorable Ephraim Tyler Tiddler, Colonel Wilkinson Jones, Mrs. Baggini, Mrs. Schwartz, Mrs. Derrick, and, of course, you know the lieutenant governor."

There were more of them and my father shook hands with them all but as if he didn't know what he was doing.

The Honorable Tiddler was an old man, I mean really old. He has white hair and a white goatee and a narrow black bow tie that hangs down over his stiff white shirt front. I knew who he was because I'd seen his picture lots of times. There are a lot of colonels in Kentucky but most of them aren't as fat as Colonel Wilkinson Jones.

Miz Liz was tired so she went to her room to lie down. She made a face at me as she went. No one else was paying any attention to me and I hated the noise and all the talk and went outside. I wondered what kind of skeleton Colonel Wilkinson Jones would make.

"What is it?" I asked the the state cop who was leaning against one of the pillars.

"Maybe it's a wake," he said. "They told me to escort so I escorted. That's all I know."

The other cop didn't know either. He said he just drove where he was told and he hoped they'd stay in there long enough so he could finish the black stogie he was smoking.

I didn't really know what it was all about until I saw the newspaper that night. The picture of my mother and me was on the front page. The paper said that the Honorable

Ephraim Tyler Tiddler was not going to run for Congress again but planned to retire after 43 years of invaluable service to the community, the Commonwealth and the nation. From an inside source the newspaper said it had learned that the nomination for the Honorable Tiddler's seat had been offered to Mrs. Sybil Trewbridge and that there was every indication that she would accept. I guess the inside source was Mr. Bucknell himself. I'd seen him dodging around behind the cameraman.

The paper said that Mrs. Trewbridge had just returned from a triumph at the conference in Washington. Her acceptance of the nomination would mean that the distaff side was going to carry on the great Trewbridge tradition of public service. As president of the Ladies Union she was nationally known. A magnetic speaker, she had made herself a strong voice in national affairs and had a sympathetic understanding of the problems of youth.

There was a list of all the things my mother is president, vice president or chairwoman of. Then it said she is a mother. As there would be only token opposition at the polls in November it looked very much as if Mrs. Sybil Trewbridge would be the first Congresswoman from our part of Kentucky, and every right-thinking citizen would join the newspaper in supporting her for that high office.

16

MY UNCLE WAS DRESSED FOR TOWN AND HIS shoes shined so I knew he had just come from his office or the hospital when he came into the stable and sat on a bale of hay and watched me rubbing Stethoscope after a good run. He looked tired.

He didn't say anything for a while, then he said, "Doctor, I think we're in trouble."

When he said "doctor" I knew he wanted to talk about my father, so I gave Stethoscope a final lick, slapped him on the rump, and he went into his stall and I locked the latch because he can open it if I don't. I sat on the slanting top of the feed bin and looked at Uncle Henry.

"As you know," he said, "post-operative care can be more important than the operation itself."

"I guess so," I said.

"Your father has been doing very well. He's more like he used to be, but he could easily be pushed over again."

I nodded. I knew what he meant.

"This political thing of your mother's! The house is already over-run. It's going to be a madhouse with every jackass in Kentucky running in and out."

"There are a lot of them there right now," I said.

"There'll be more, and it will get worse. I don't want your father to hide in his books again or in his job at the college. So what are we going to do?"

I knew right away because I'd been thinking about it while I rubbed down Stethoscope and I'd been thinking about it a lot before that. "Take him to the Derby," I said.

117

My uncle looked at me as if he thought I had lost my mind.

"Take him out of one madhouse and put him into a bigger one! You know as well as I that excitement is what we must avoid."

"There aren't any books there and the jackasses don't show so much," I said. "He wouldn't get excited about the Derby. He likes horses but just to ride and be with. He went with me on Scalpel Sunday."

"He did! I told him not to ride until I said so, though Scalpel needs the exercise."

"It didn't make him tired. He liked it. He liked it a lot."

"That's fortunate."

"He doesn't even know what horses are running in the Derby or which is the favorite. I heard him talking to people in Berea. I don't think he even knows what the Winter Book is."

My uncle laughed. "I'm sure he doesn't."

"He wouldn't get excited at the Derby. He'd just watch the other people get excited. He'd see and hear the crowds but it wouldn't have anything to do with him so he'd just like being there and away from home the way it is now."

My uncle looked funny. "You know him, don't you?"

"Known him all my life," I said, "and I know him better now."

My uncle got up from the hay and went over and straightened some of the tack on the pegs. Then he walked down and looked at Scalpel. He turned around.

"What was your medical school, doctor? Know what I'm going to do? I'm going to help your mother." He grinned at me. "Come on. I'll drop you off home. I'm going downtown but tell Miz Liz I'll be there at dinner."

At dinner he told my mother that it was inefficient trying to run her campaign from the house. She had to be available to her assistants and to the public at all times. He'd found a vacant store downtown that would make ideal campaign headquarters. He'd pay the rent as his contribution to her election.

My mother was really pleased.

"Henry, how kind! And I thought you were not taking my public life seriously. You don't know how perfectly this fits in with my plans. I've been bursting to tell all of you the news. Dear Hamilton is coming home to run my campaign. Of course, I've planned all along that he will be my secretary when we go to Washington. I already have my eye on a darling little house in Georgetown."

"That girl gone?" asked Miz Liz.

"I'm sure I don't know," said my mother impatiently.

"There are two rooms fitted up as living quarters and a bath behind the store," said Uncle Henry.

"Perfect! Hamilton will live there. He is above material things."

I thought Hamilton wouldn't need the bath much or the girl either. If there was a new girl she'd probably be like the old one. I didn't say anything though. I was watching my father. His face didn't show anything, but he wasn't eating. When he saw I was looking at him he looked away.

They put new telephones in the store and banners over the door and pasted posters all over the windows. One was a big copy of the news photograph of my mother and me. My mother went there every morning and stayed until late at night. She was hardly ever home, not even when we had dinner in the dining room. A few people like reporters and Congressmen and postmen with special delivery letters still came to the house, but most of the people and the telephone calls went to the "Campaign Headquarters of Sybil Trewbridge, Our Next Representative in Congress," which is what the big sign over the store says. I went there a few times and saw a lot of girls answering the telephones and folding advertisements into long envelopes and licking them or typing or things like that.

One day there was a man there in a dark suit, a white shirt with a button-down collar and a striped tie talking to some other men. He seemed to be giving orders, and they were listening. He was clean-shaven except for a big mustache. I wondered who he was. Then he turned a little and I saw it was Hamilton!

He was talking to the other men as if he knew what he was talking about, and he looked good. I found out later that in New York my mother had bought him three suits and a lot of shirts and things and that he had had his hair cut and styled by a woman hairdresser, but it wasn't only that. He looked happy. He looked sure of himself and happy.

One other day — it was awful — I found my mother there alone. I don't know where all the others were, but she was just sitting at her desk looking off at nothing.

"Yes?" she said when she heard someone come in.

"Nothing," I said.

She jumped up and ran around her desk and grabbed me and hugged me tight and kissed me hard.

"Vergil! I've been worried about you! Things are so frightful here and there's so much to do I just don't. . ."

I pulled myself away. "That's all right," I said.

She stood and looked at me for a minute. "You're growing!" she said as if she'd never noticed before.

"A little," I said.

Her hands started out toward me again, but she drew them back and went and sat behind her desk and looked up at me.

"I —," she said. "I —"

"I wish I were old enough to vote for you!" I said before I could stop myself.

Then my mother began to cry. She didn't make any noise. Just tears came and rolled down her cheeks. She didn't pay any attention to them.

"Sometimes we have to live beyond our own little lives," she said slowly. "Sometimes I think I can't, but I have to try. I *have* to!"

"I know," I said.

"I *have* to do things. You understand, don't you?"

"Yes."

"Perhaps I can even help make the world a little better." My mother was sort of pleading, and her eyes were looking right into mine.

I didn't want her to cry any more, and she kept looking at me when I didn't answer right away, and she looked kind of hopeful so I said, "Maybe, but I like it all right the way it is."

"Do you — do think your father — that is, does he understand a little too?"

"I think he's right proud of you," I said as quickly as I could, and then I was glad I said it because my mother looked really happy.

"Oh, thank you, Vergil" she said. "Thank you!"

She smiled then, and she reached for her handbag to get her handkerchief and touched her eyes with it. Then she put the handkerchief away and closed the bag and put it back on her desk where it had been. She looked away from me and out the window into the street. There were cars going by.

"Vergil, you *know* I love you."

"That's all right," I said again.

Until now I've never told anybody about that afternoon. I didn't go back to the store again, and I tried not to think about it. I had other things to think about anyway.

I don't think my mother knew that Derby was almost here. I knew though, and I kept waiting for Uncle Henry to tell me. Finally he did.

"I've been thinking over your suggested therapy, doctor," he said. "It doesn't make sense, but in my limited experience it's the things that don't make sense that sometimes make the most sense. You follow me?"

"No," I said.

"We're going to the Derby. Your father, Miss Susan, you, and I — that is if somebody doesn't decide to need emergency surgery at the last minute and if Dr. Roland will look after my present patients."

"That's good," I said.

Miz Liz said it was a waste of time and money and a lot of tomfoolery. She knows all about the Derby. Away back before I was born she saw Man O'War win it, and she saw him a lot more times at the Ridley Farm. She says that other horses are just horses but that Man O'War was Big Red himself and that they stopped making real horses after him. She said she knew better than to go traipsing off to Louisville just to see some three-year old platers pretend they knew how to run a mile and a quarter.

I laughed at her, and my father did too, but she didn't care.

First I decided I'd wear my jodhpurs and boots but then I decided that would be showing off. Owners don't go to the Jockey Club dressed that way. I decided I'd look as much like my father and my uncle as I could because you can't look better than that. We'd be gone most of a week so, of course, I had to take other things like my madder sweater and some extra flannel trousers and my toothbrush and pajamas. I had my bag all packed four days before we had to go.

The time went slowly, and just the day before we were going Uncle Henry had three operations and one of his hospital patients got worse and he had to stay there most of the night. It worried me because we were going in his car. My father could not drive that far yet. I needn't have worried. My uncle is always on time — that's one of the things I have learned from him — and he was on time that morning.

His big car is a good one. Soon we were running smoothly down the highways through magnolias and rhododendron and laurel all in bloom, my uncle and Miss Susan in front and my father and I in back.

My father was looking at the spring this year all right. He never took his eyes off the countryside we passed, and he didn't say much. He just smiled at me once in a while. He looked content and his eyes were lighted.

Derby time isn't just Derby time. It's Kentucky time. All Kentucky is alive, sweet-smelling and beautiful when the horses are running at Churchill Downs. A million people come to look at about twenty horses. You couldn't get a million horses to come and look at twenty people or even thirty. They don't care, but the people do. They come from everywhere. They fill the hotels or stay with their friends or sleep in their cars or in all-night movies. They camp on the infield at Churchill Downs or just walk up and down South Fourth Street. Probably some of them don't go to bed at all.

The traffic got heavier as we got closer to Louisville; then it got worse, and by the time we reached Broadway, which goes east and west the length of the city, it was almost impossible. The cars were full of people laughing and talking and waving. Finally we reached the Brown Hotel at the corner of Broadway and Fourth Street. That's where we always go. My uncle had telephoned away ahead, and he can always get reservations because he knows the people there.

The sidewalks were jammed all around the hotel and the lobby was packed. Bellhops were running all over the place carrying bags and paging people. Lines waited before the elevators which kept running up and down. My father, who can look over the heads of most people, looked confused but kind of pleased as my uncle registered and took care of things at the desk.

Derby is the first Saturday in May. As the time gets closer it seems as if people all hold their breath and then let it out in one big gasp when the week comes. They come in the big regular planes or in their own little ones, on the trains, but mostly in their cars, and they come for the good time of the year.

My father lay down on one of the beds as soon as we got into our room, but I could see the heads of the people and the tops of the cars on Fourth Street from our window and hear the noise so, after he fell asleep, I went down in the elevator and out through the lobby into the crowd. You could hardly move on the sidewalk. People who hadn't seen one another for a long time, probably a year, were shaking hands or dodging across the street between the cars when they spotted someone they knew on the other side.

Television sets were flashing race pictures in shop windows and radios were shouting over loudspeakers. I dodged and brushed my way toward the big Ohio River, which isn't far, just the other side of Jefferson, and tried to see everything I could but I couldn't see much because of all the people.

I suppose New York and Chicago are bigger and noisier and I know Atlanta is, but I don't think any of them seem bigger or more crowded than Fourth Street in Louisville at Derby time. There were people who looked rich and people who didn't, and people who looked like my brother and the girl did at Christmas. There were some just going about their business, but they had a hard time in the crowd. I stopped at one of the places where you can pay and send a copy of the big special Derby edition of the *Courier-Journal* and made out the blank and paid to send one to Miz Liz.

I didn't go all the way to the river because I knew my father wouldn't sleep long and might be afraid I'd got lost. He was just waking when I got back and didn't know I'd been out.

"Afraid I dozed off," he said.

"It's pretty exciting," I said.

"It's supposed to be, and it's a good thing to get your blood stirred up once in a while."

"You're not supposed to stir yours too much," I said.

He was sitting up and leaning on his elbow and he laughed at me. All of a sudden he looked young, younger even than my uncle. He looked around. "Strange," he said, "a hotel room and I feel more at home than when we were home. I used to be in Louisville often."

Then he looked very serious. "We can be very proud of your mother," he said firmly.

"I am," I said, and I meant it.

124

"You must understand about her. She knows what she wants and she gets things done, important things perhaps, in a way I never could and I'm afraid you never will. She has to."

"I know," I said. "She'll be in the history books some day, won't she?"

"She may well be." Then my father looked at me hard. "You really do understand, don't you." He sounded a little surprised but he looked as if he was relieved that he had got something important off his mind.

"I guess so," I said.

Then he changed again. He jumped up and said, "Let's go out!"

I didn't tell him I had been and I was glad. We walked down Fourth Street the way I had gone and he pointed out different buildings and places to me. He walked free and loose and easily and people didn't bump into us. He sniffed as if he liked the smell of the air. I tried it but all I got was the smell of burning oil from one of the five-and-dime stores where they were roasting cashew nuts. It was a sickening smell and I didn't like it. Probably the air is better when you're tall like my father.

"Get your Derby souvenir! Get your Derby souvenir!" The hawkers were selling banners and buttons and noise makers but we didn't want any.

There was a crowd in front of the Seelbach where the racing people go, and there was another crowd by the Brown when we got back. One of the first things we saw was some people talking to my uncle in the lobby. Wherever he goes people know him. Miss Susan saw us and smiled at me and a half dozen other people smiled back hoping she meant them.

That night we went to a Derby dinner at the house of some kinfolk out near St. Matthews. The next morning we went to a Derby breakfast at a big stone house on Cherokee Road in the Highlands. Probably it was a good thing as the restaurants downtown were so crowded you couldn't get into them.

There were a lot of people at the breakfast, all making a fuss over my father and I could see he liked it. After a while I asked him if I could and he said yes so I went out by myself and walked for a while in Cherokee Park. It was quiet there. The grass was green and the redbud and dogwood were all in blossom. The newspaper said that Cherokee and Shawnee Park at the other end of the city looked like fairyland for the Derby so I guess they did.

We went back to the Brown, and Miss Susan met some people she knew and my father and my uncle talked to them so I went for another walk. This time I went up Broadway as far as Beargrass Creek. It wasn't so crowded on Broadway so I could really look around, and I liked it.

We went to a Derby luncheon at a restaurant with more kinfolk and friends, and it was from there we went to the track.

That isn't easy on Derby Day. I could have walked faster than our cab, but I was glad I didn't have to. I know there are that many people but I'd never seen them all together at one time. The crowd could smother you, but we got through the gates without too much trouble and the mob inside was something. Finally we got to our seats in the clubhouse enclosure and it wasn't so bad there.

People were sitting studying their racing cards so as to place their bets at the long line of windows. More men hurried over to shake hands with my father and uncle and look at Miss Susan, and every one of them knew which horse would win, place or show in every race except the Derby. They asked us about that but my father only laughed and shook his head and my uncle said he was going to bet on the horse whose jockey's silks matched the color of Miss Susan's eyes, but he didn't mean it.

People don't pay much attention to the early races Derby Day and I didn't care about them. My father and I walked around to the paddock to watch the horses and their handlers. The horses were beautiful, all of them. I could never make up my mind which would be the fastest in any race. My father said he was going back to our seats to see the parade to the post for the first race, but I didn't care who won that one so I asked him if I could look around some more. He said all right but not to get lost.

I knew where I was going. I wanted to see where some day Stethoscope might be staying. It was a long way out and there was no crowd there. I kept going toward the long, low row of stables and no one stopped me. It was quieter here. There was just the good stable smell of dung, ammonia, leather, liniment and horse. A few grooms and handlers were working around just as if there were no Kentucky Derby coming up anywhere near. Horses poked their heads out of the open top halves of doors closed at the bottom and looked at me. A man was sitting with his chair tipped back against the wall the way they do near one of them.

"Like horses, kid?" he said.

"Yes," I said.

A roar went up so I knew the first race had started. We both listened a minute. Then the man shrugged. "Nothin' no good in that race. Got a horse somewhere?" he asked me.

I'd learned how much trouble you get into by telling people things, like the ecology and the skeleton at school, so I said, "I have a dog."

"A black and white one? Dalmations, they call 'em. They're good around horses."

"Mine's a beagle. His name is Cicero." After I spoke I remembered the little boy and girl and their poodle-terrier and I thought I sounded as little as they are.

"His name is *what*?"

I told him again.

The man let his chair tip forward so that all its feet were on the ground. "Hey, Joe!" he called to another man in old riding breeches but no boots and even unfastened at the bottoms who was going by with a forkful of hay. "This kid's got a dog named Cicero!" He couldn't even say it right.

The second man stopped. He wasn't very big and he was a little bowlegged. He'd been a jockey or an exercise boy once. He looked me over.

"That's all right, kid," he said. "Some of these horses is dogs, real dogs." He laughed.

I knew what he meant and I liked him, but I said, "I know. I heard them barking."

The man with the hay laughed again but the first man didn't. He looked at me sort of puzzled. Then he said, "Hey, you better git out of here, kid. You're botherin' me. No one ain't supposed to be here anyways."

My uncle held up a fistful of money when I got back to the enclosure. He'd won on the first two races, and one was a long-shot and paid off plenty.

"My diagnosis was good," he told me. He nodded toward my father. "So was yours."

My father was watching everything quietly, enjoying the sounds, the color, the whole spectacle. Suddenly he got up, waved at me, and went away. We watched him go toward the mutuel windows.

"I hope he doesn't lose too much," said my uncle laughing.

It takes a long time for the Derby to come. It is late afternoon and the sun is dropping before the other races are over. There is a great sigh all over Churchill Downs and then a hush. The horn sounds and the slow parade to the post starts, the entries prancing, their jocks in their brilliant silks holding them under tight rein, the stablemates loping alongside. They reach the post and the stablemates trot off the track fast. The starters are getting the fastest three-year olds in the world into position. One breaks out of the gate and three men push him back.

We were all watching through our binoculars. I'd brought

mine and I could see everything. I grabbed my father's arm and Miss Susan grabbed my uncle's and held tight.

"They're off!"

It takes only about two minutes, but it's the longest two minutes of the year. I watched the break, then the fight for position along the rail, then the three leaders. The third jockey was digging in his spurs and flailing with his whip. I knew it didn't hurt. Horses don't feel it in the excitement, but they do afterward. I wouldn't want any professional jock digging spikes into Stethoscope and raising welts on him. I was glad when the first two horses left the third behind.

The screaming and shouting was deafening, but I didn't make a sound. I couldn't as one horse led by a neck, then by a half length, then by a length and a half at the wire. Some people screamed and jumped up and down for joy. Others made faces of disgust and tore up their betting tickets. I looked up to see how my father liked it. He was gone.

I shouted to make my uncle hear. "Where is he? Where is he?"

"I don't think I want to say," said my uncle unhappily.

I saw my father coming back then. I wanted to run to him but I couldn't because everybody was standing watching the winner move into the winner's circle and the big wreath of roses being placed over his head. My father was smiling and waving at us.

When he reached me the first thing he did was hand me ten dollars.

"I bet two dollars for you and ten for myself," he said. He'd bet to win against the favorite and his horse had paid ten dollars for two, which are good odds.

He gave my uncle and Miss Susan a dollar each. "That's all your advice was worth," he said. "Rather it's a dollar more than it was worth!"

He was laughing and happy. He'd let go. He'd *really* let go! He looked strong and handsome, as handsome as my

uncle. You'd think he'd never read a book or had a heart attack at all.

My uncle took his dollar and folded it carefully and slipped
it into the breast pocket of his jacket. "This is worth more
than a dollar to us, Verge," he said to me.

The band was playing "My Old Kentucky Home," and the
crowd was singing. Miss Susan was singing with them and I
could see my father's lips moving with the words as if he
sang to himself. I couldn't sing because you get a lump in
your throat and the goose pimples jump cold on your arms,
and for a minute you can't see right well.

I decided I'd give a dollar of my ten to my mother for her
campaign.

17

ONE GOOD THING ABOUT THE DERBY IS IT REMINDS you that it's getting time to plant. If you don't get your things into the ground between then and Confederate Memorial Day you might as well forget them.

I suppose nothing is ever all good and in Louisville I'd found out something that wasn't. I'd weighed myself on a machine out at the track, and I'd gained weight. I suspected something else so I went down to my uncle's office and measured myself on the thing he has there. I'd grown almost another inch.

Miss Susan said wasn't that fine and some day I'd be as tall as my uncle. Well, I didn't think it was that fine. If I kept on growing, I'd never be able to ride Stethoscope in a race next year, the Derby or even a quarter-mile track at a county fair. I'd be too big. I'd even be too big to exercise him right for competition.

Actually I didn't feel too badly after what I'd seen through my glasses at the Derby and what I knew anyway. If a horse wants to race you can hand-ride him and win, but most jockeys don't know that. Stethoscope wasn't going to get beaten by any jockey hungry for prize money. I didn't want his hocks fired either, the way they sometimes do with a racing horse so he will run trying to get away from the pain in his legs.

Stethoscope loves to race himself or the wind or Scalpel or a butterfly if he sees one or Cicero any time, but I'm not sure he'd like the noise and the crowds, especially some of the kinds of people you see around racing stables, any more than I do. He doesn't have to win any Derbies to be Stethoscope to me. I talked to my uncle about it and he said I was right. He'd not ask a horse to do anything he wouldn't do himself. It sounded as if he were saying he wouldn't run in the Derby himself, but I knew what he meant.

This doesn't mean I stopped training Stethoscope and working him out. He was getting faster and faster, and I was riding better. My father was right too. I ride better in my jodhpurs and boots. Stethoscope sniffed them the first time. It took a while for them to smell like me. Now he's used to them, and I am. One day my uncle clocked us over a quarter mile.

"Not bad," he said, "Not bad at all."

"Then you think maybe — ?"

"I think you won't stop hoping. Care for another professional confidence, doctor?"

"Yes."

"People have pituitaries and adrenalin and a few more glands and juices. Without them they wouldn't be much better off than that skeleton of yours. It's why they fight wars and probably always will, which is too bad, but it's also why your father fought his way back and your mother is hell-bent on election."

"I see," I said. I did a little.

"There's another part. They hope, and while they're alive you can't stop them. I could show you where the pituitary was or should have been on that skeleton but I've never been able to locate hope anywhere in the frame or the carcass. You've studied the skeleton. Did you find it?"

"No," I said.

"I was afraid of that, but you know what it can do. We even helped it along a little, didn't we?"

"I think we did."

My uncle smiled at me, not the charming smile he gave my mother but the one he uses with my father and me. "So why don't you go plant your tobacco," he said.

He was right about that too. The ground was warmed. Mr. Kinney had had my quarter acre ploughed and harrowed when he had my uncle's fields done. It's on a hillside with a good exposure. The tobacco settings had come and were waiting in their boxes in the shed. It took a whole crew a couple of days to plant my uncle's black burley. He always has a good crop.

The next Saturday my father drove me out to the farm, and I had a crew too, Margaret Hobart. She was home because her school in Virginia closes early, and she'd come to work.

It's a funny thing about Margaret Hobart. When she wants to do something, she can really do it, usually better than most people. She went right at it. She did exactly as I told her and she did it right. What you do is mark your rows then walk along them dropping the plants a couple of feet apart. Then you take a small peg pointed at one end, twist a hole in the earth, poke in the plant, and pull the soil around it.

We laid out the rows, then went back, and Margaret Hobart began to plant one row and I worked along beside her planting the next.

"Isn't it wonderful about your mother," she said. "We were so excited when we got the news in Richmond! Just think, you'll have a Congressman for a mother! Congressperson, I mean."

"Keep the plant up straight," I said. "Don't tip it to one side."

"Probably she'll be the first woman President."

"Who says so?"

"Everybody! If I weren't going to be an actress I'd probably go into the Senate myself. Women are going to be in charge now, you know."

"I thought they always were," I said. I twisted a new hole in the ground.

"And Hamilton is a big help to her," Margaret Hobart said as she straightened a set. "My mother says he is just won-

133

derful, and they looked wonderful on television the other night. Where are they now?"

"I don't know."

My mother and my brother were out testing the grass roots. That's what my mother said. They were going to every town talking to mayors and people like that and shaking hands. I wondered how the babies felt when Hamilton kissed them. He'll never get my vote by kissing me.

My mother was hardly ever home now. If she wasn't making speeches somewhere, she was in Washington to confer with her advisors or in Frankfort talking to party leaders. Hamilton was always with her. I think he had found himself helping my mother in his new suits.

It was a warm day, and the sun was getting high. Margaret Hobart brushed the sweat from her forehead and left a dirty streak. She was wearing shorts, and her legs were pretty dirty too. She had kicked off her loafers to squinch the warm earth between her toes. I knew how good it felt because I'd taken off my shoes too.

We weren't just talking. We were working hard. Margaret Hobart kept up with me, and we were more than half way down the two rows. I didn't want her to say later that I had made her work too hard so I said, "Let's take a break."

Sitting there on the ground in the sun we could look down and see my father and Uncle Henry inspecting a horse. My father had decided to get one of his own so that he could ride with my uncle and me. They'd looked at several but didn't want them. A dealer had brought this one to show.

My father and my uncle and I had talked it all over nights. They talked about Palominos and Morgans and Apaloosas and Quarter Horses and I don't know what other kinds, but that was just because we like to talk about horses. I knew my father would never really get anything but a Kentucky Thoroughbred. He'd already decided on a name — Colophon. It was a Thoroughbred they were looking at now, and I felt pretty sure my father would take him. I knew the horse, and he was a good one.

Always curious, Stethoscope had walked over to see what they were doing and what the new horse looked like. Probably he hoped they'd ask for his opinion. Scalpel was standing in the shade under a maple ignoring the whole business. That's the difference between them. I pointed it out to Margaret Hobart.

She didn't look down at the horses. She looked at me instead. I guess she was still thinking about Hamilton and the way he used to be because she said, "You don't have any trouble with your identity, do you?"

"What?"

"You always know who you are."

"I'm just me, that's all," I said. "Let's go back to work."

We finished the rows we were on and started two more. Our backs began to ache, and the palms of our right hands were sore from twisting the pegs into the ground. Margaret Hobart got a blister on hers. She said it was nothing, but I wouldn't let her plant any more. If the blister broke and it got dirt in it, it might get infected, and her mother would say look what I'd done now and tell my father because she wouldn't be able to reach my mother, and he might worry.

Margaret Hobart just lay on her stomach watching for a time. Then she turned over on her back and looked at some little clouds that were going by on their way toward Lexington. She sat up when I finished and came and sat down next to me on the hillside. We could see my uncle trotting the new horse, trying it out while my father and the dealer watched.

My tobacco was in, and I was glad of that. I was tired and sweaty and dirty but sort of content. It was good to see my father and my uncle and the horses in the pasture and to look over the fields to the woods and the branch where the sun was sparkling on the water. I didn't want to move.

Margaret Hobart was looking at it all too. Then she said something I didn't hear.

"What?"

She repeated it. " 'Every year its springtime.' It's from a poem I know."

"Oh!"

Cicero came. He was panting, and his tongue and muzzle were all dirt because he had been digging. He flopped down beside us, and Margaret Hobart patted him and stroked one of his ears. She held it up.

"His ears are even bigger than yours," she said as if she had just discovered something.

"Thank you for helping me," I said.

"I liked it," she said.

She was still looking out over the farm. She's quieter since she came back from Richmond. She's taller too, and now she has her hair just brushed back and tied with a black ribbon. It looks good.

"I suppose we'd better go down," I said. "I want to know if they bought Colophon, and I'm hungry and thirsty. Aren't you?"

"A little." Margaret Hobart looked at me, and she was very serious. "Verge, are you in love with me?"

"No."

"Lots of men are going to be pretty soon. I just wanted to know whether it's started yet."

"Not yet," I said.

"Race you to the stable!" she said, and she was gone.